Beauty and the Billionaire Beast

MARIA HOAGLAND

ALSO BY MARIA HOAGLAND

BILLIONAIRE CLASSICS

Beauty and the Billionaire Beast

Her App, a Match, and the Billionaire

Falling for Her Billionaire Best Friend

The Matchmaker's Billionaire

COBBLE CREEK SERIES

The Inventive Bride

The Practically Romantic Groom

The Combustible Engagement

ROMANCE RENOVATIONS SERIES

Home for the Holidays

Kayaks & Kisses

New Year's Resolutions

Love for Keeps

Santa Cam

Still Time

The ReModel Marriage

Beauty and the Billionaire Beast

MARIA HOAGLAND

RED LEAVES PRESS

2017

© 2017 by Maria Hoagland

All rights reserved.

No part of this book may be reproduced in any form or by any electronic or mechanical means, including information storage and retrieval systems, without written permission from the author, except for the use of brief quotations in a book review.

This is a work of fiction. The characters, incidents, and dialogue are products of the author's imagination and not meant to be construed as real.

Published by Red Leaves Press, an imprint of Sisters Ink Publishing, Kuna, ID.

ISBN-13: 9781700484055

ISBN-10: 1-7004-8405-2

LCCN: 2017908789

Cover design © 2019 by Red Leaves Press

Author photograph by Erin Summerill © 2015

Printed in the United States of America

To Curtis, my very own fairy-tale prince who has never been a beast and has always made me feel like a beauty. I love sharing our enchanted love story and look forward to adventures with you for eternity.

CHAPTER 1

The whisper of a breeze shouldn't have been enough to lift the corners of Emma Treager's sketchbook, nevertheless, something disturbed its thick pages and caused her pencil to roll. Her light summer skirt swirled around the leg of her wrought iron chair, lifting the hem and threatening to expose more thigh than she was comfortable showing. In a slight panic, Emma trapped the skirt with one hand and reached for the pencil with the other, leaning too much to the right. The combination of wobbly chair legs, uneven flagstone, and her off-centered weight caused the chair to tip, and for a split second, Emma was certain she was about to crash onto the unforgiving ground.

A pair of strong hands from behind steadied her.

"Good morning, miss. Allow me to get that for you." The man's voice was refined but young, calm despite her near-fatal fall, and . . . safe. It was as if he saved tumbling women on a regular basis.

From over her shoulder, he leaned forward—his arm grazing hers, commanding her full attention—and retrieved the pencil. Crouched to her side for a better reach, he turned to Emma, his left hand on the back of her chair, his right hand offering what she'd lost. "Here you are."

His face, on the same level as hers, was so close she could feel the fresh rush of mint from his breath. His chiseled features were startlingly handsome, like a marble statue straight out of an Italian garden, but there was something else about him that caught Emma's interest. He obviously had great DNA, a family gene jackpot, though he clearly took good care of himself. You didn't get a chest like his by chance or laziness, but the perfect symmetry of his face, the strong chin, and the lake-blue irises didn't speak of who he really was, just what he was lucky enough to inherit. It was the look on his face that revealed his character. His eyes were soft with concern, and one corner of his mouth quirked up in an air of mischievousness. There was definitely more to him than his features, and she felt a desire to find out what it was.

Emma swallowed, allowing herself to catch her

breath, passing it off as a side effect of the near fall. "Thank you."

As she set the pencil beside the notebook and straightened it, Emma saw the man's eyes fall onto her sketch. Although her gut reaction was to slam the pages closed, she fought the urge and allowed him to look. She was a professional, and she should be proud of her work.

Live Oak Lane was by far the most picturesque plantation she'd visited on her trip through Louisiana's cobwebbed corners of history. Today's setting was perfect—almost too perfect, really—but inspiring enough that she'd wanted to sketch the details for future reference. Emma had been seated alone on the patio at the side of the house, the sole visitor at one of the several café tables. She'd carefully chosen her spot with the best view of the property. An allée of ancient live oak trees led to the front of the palatial house. Closer and more interesting to her were the immaculate gardens, sculpted carefully with flowers and shrubs of varying heights, colors, and textures.

The gardens were lovely, which was why she was sketching them, but there was also a falseness to them. Things were just too planned, too contrived. She wondered how many gardeners the property employed and if they had a need for a full-time historic landscape architect, though there was absolutely nothing she would change if she held the position.

"You're talented."

The man's simple statement left Emma blushing at the compliment. "Thank you." Normally she could take praise as well as anyone, but coming from him, it warmed her through.

As the man stood, Emma squared her shoulders, trying to quiet the pounding heart that was more than adrenaline from a near fall. She clasped her hands and set them on the book. Should she invite him to sit with her? An awkward silence fell between them, and she worked to come up with something to say.

He turned, but she wasn't ready for him to go. "Is this your first visit to Live Oak Lane?" The words rushed out, probably leaving him with no doubt of her intent. She felt the blush deepen. Her traitorous pale skin turned on her time and again.

He stopped mid-step. "No, I've been here several times. It's always nice, but they've done some recent work, so I wanted to check it out."

"Oh." She hadn't known anything about the place other than it was the top result every time she'd searched the internet for Louisiana plantations. The man seemed to know more about the property and its history than she did.

"Enjoy your visit." He turned to step away again, but hesitated and turned back around.

The romantic in her hoped he'd ask her name or sit down and strike up a conversation, but that was ridiculous. Things like that didn't happen in real life, and if they did, she'd be wary of an overly friendly man who picked up strange women at tourist traps.

"Live Oak Lane might be the grandest of the area's plantations; it certainly is the best dressed. *Currently.*" He said this last bit under his breath. "It's the right one if you're into movie-set quality, but if you're interested in history, you might want to check out some of the lesser-known plantations."

Surprised, Emma didn't respond quickly enough, finding herself instead watching this perfect specimen of a man retreat, his well-cut slacks and tailored dress shirt outlining his broad shoulders, confidence exuding from him. In that moment, he felt like a vision on some higher plane than she could ever attain, and for that reason, she sat, unable to ask his retreating form, though he might have the exact information she was seeking.

"Whew! He's gone." The waitress who'd stepped outside, ostensibly to clear tables, stood with her arms folded, doing exactly what Emma was doing—watching the man leave.

"Finally," a man's voice agreed. Emma turned to see

her tour guide from earlier leaning against the doorframe. His eyes were fixed on the pretty, petite waitress at his side. "What was he even doing here?" the tour guide grumped.

"Spying, no doubt." Now that Emma's rescuer was out of sight, the waitress began wiping the already-clean tables. "Though I have no idea why he would even try. I hear Indigo Pointe is practically in ruins, and you know as well as I do he won't be able to get anyone to work for him—not after the way he's been treating employees. Did you hear he fired Charlie's uncle last week after twenty years of service? Twenty years the man worked there, and then—no warning, no explanation, not even a replacement—the guy was thrown out. And not very nicely, I heard."

"What do you expect?" The young man straightened chairs under café tables as the waitress washed, his long fingers choking the top of each chair in frustration. "His family's been like that for generations. They take and take from this community, their friends and neighbors, on top of making all that money off the backs of our ancestors. They're incorrigible."

Emma wondered how much of their conversation should be taken at face value. It sounded like a cocktail of sour grapes, gossip, and conjecture, but there was usually a seed of truth to every complaint. Perhaps she was lucky she hadn't convinced Mr. Gorgeous to stay and chat. Despite what these two said about the deplorable conditions at Indigo Pointe, she was willing to visit the man's plantation. It could be the one she was searching for.

From the moment she'd seen the photos online, Emma had known that Live Oak Lane wasn't it. Major things were off—the placement and style of the stairs, for starters. That was why she'd put it last on her list to tour, but she hadn't wanted to return to Oregon without exhausting every remote possibility. She'd been determined that somehow, somewhere, she would discover the mysterious plantation described in her great-grandfather's journal. She was hoping for pictures as a hundredth-birthday gift to her grandfather.

Indigo Pointe Plantation. Maybe she finally found her lead.

CHAPTER 2

After leaving Live Oak Lane, Emma set out for Indigo Pointe, but the internet was marginally helpful and her GPS even less so.

"Ugh!" Emma shook her head and turned the car around. "Forget it!" She might as well head back into town.

Disappointment churned in her stomach. Surrendering her last hope at finding a link between her great-grandfather and the Louisiana plantation of his childhood didn't sit well. After two unsuccessful passes down the road, Emma was ready to convince herself the property wasn't worth any more frustration.

The third time she'd almost driven past the entrance, a flash in her periphery caught her attention. Slowing the car to a crawl, she searched for the source but saw nothing out of the ordinary other than the trees and rolling hills so different from the desert climate of her farming town of Nyssa. The only places Eastern Oregon had that were green were contentiously irrigated, forcing nature to go from barren to agricultural hub. Here, the windy road was bordered with native Cypress trees and swamp grass adorned with a tangle of goldenrod.

There. She saw it again. A shimmering illusion like fairy dust. She shook her head, knowing her mother would laugh it off as Emma's love of all things curious and unexplainable. Emma stopped on the shoulder and then rolled her window down to get a better view. There wasn't anything wrong with believing in a little magic.

Emma scrutinized the vegetation across the road where the shimmer had been, and noticed a wrought iron gate almost overtaken by a bank of aggressive evergreen shrubs.

The most ornamented Emma could ever remember seeing, the gate had it all: curlicues, scrolls, circles, flowers, arrows, finials, and . . . was that a lion or a horse rearing up on the top? Sandwiched between fifteen-foot white-plastered pillars, the black gate portended some majestic, yet possibly sinister structure.

Curious for a better look, Emma got out of her car

and crossed the road, the tingle of adventure running down her spine. Knowing she wouldn't see anything at eye level through the thick of the bushes, she lay on her stomach where the branches were thinner. As she stuck both hands through the gate's bars and pushed back the scratchy branches, she was rewarded with a view of exactly what she'd been searching for. Across a large expanse of patchy grass sat a stately antebellum mansion with thick columns and two distinct staircases swooping up to a second-story balcony. This had to be the plantation her great-grandfather had described in his journal.

She took in the rest of the house. While the bones of the structure were regal, the roof was a bit saggy, the plaster off-color and patchy, the green trim and shutters faded. Surrounding it were overgrown and ill-chosen plants. The place could be as beautiful and elegant as any of the other plantations she'd toured, if only it had a little TLC and a lot of money.

She needed to find a way in.

Standing, Emma brushed off and returned to her car. After starting the engine, she inched forward, looking for the turnoff that had to be around somewhere. Since the main gate was far from functional, there had to be access for the property owners somewhere else close by. A couple hundred yards later and around a bend, her eyes caught an entrance. With all the ivy overtaking the fence, it was no wonder she'd missed the faded wooden sign that read *Historic Indigo Pointe Plantation*.

Before overhearing the conversation at Live Oak Lane, Emma had never even come across that name during her research, and she thought she'd been plenty thorough. Her whole life she'd had a secret fascination with Louisiana plantations despite the fact that she grew up in the West, about as far away from anything Southern as a family could get. They didn't even drink iced tea, for goodness' sake.

Never once had anyone hinted at a family connection with the place until a few months ago. When visiting at Christmas, Emma had asked Opa for the story behind his antique writing secretary, a unique wooden box that had always fascinated her.

"I don't rightly know," Opa admitted, regret pinching his words. "It's been in the family for generations as far as I know, but I've always wanted to know more."

He then had pulled out his father's journal, a hand-bound, leather-wrapped book full of elegantly penned words and sketches.

"I don't suppose I've ever told you about the Treager family treasure, have I?"

Emma had been bursting with anticipation, knowing something great was about to happen.

Opa leaned forward like someone about to share a

ghost story over a campfire. "Family lore is that there's a treasure back at the family plantation." He patted the book. "My father's journal mentions it time and again, but no one was ever able to find it."

"Wait." Emma had held up a hand to pause the conversation. "A plantation? As in the South somewhere?"

Opa nodded slowly. "All's I remember is that it's in Louisiana somewheres. I can't remember much. We moved to Oregon when I was little and never went back." He laughed derisively. "Seems to me this bit about the treasure is just some family story, made up for entertainment on a long winter night. If there'd been any real treasure, someone would have found it." He handed the book to Emma. "But why don't you see if you can find something?"

That was when, with Opa's hundredth birthday party only a few months away, Emma had decided on her gift to him. She would fill in the gaps on his family tree, and maybe, if she was lucky, she would find some family stories along the way, including the origin of the box or even the treasure. The thought gave her chills.

And now, here she was, ready to set foot on the very same plantation her great-grandfather must have seen. Anticipation bubbled inside her.

Unlike the locked ornamental gate directly in front of the plantation house, the simple chain-link gate at this side entrance was open, tepidly welcoming visitors to the property. At least, she hoped it was the same property. Instead of driving up to the main house, the entrance led to what was probably an office. The simple clapboard structure, possibly antebellum itself, was small but in decent repair. It was fronted by a potholed, graveled parking lot. Here and there, clumps of stubborn grass and weeds thrived despite being crushed over and over. Two cars were parked in front of a dilapidated wheelchair ramp that led to a door with an *Open* sign. Emma sighed with relief. At least she wasn't trespassing.

She parked and walked toward the door with purpose, her footsteps amplified on the wooden floorboards. The door stuck as she forced it open into a small cluster of rooms. The room straight ahead was museum-like with old tools and other relics in glass cases. The room to her right was a small store with books and souvenir trinkets. The main room was weighted down with a long wooden counter, behind which a friendly face looked up from a book. The woman wore a peasant blouse with an abstract emerald-colored design woven through, a matching scarf wound around her head.

"Welcome to Indigo Pointe Plantation." Despite the warm greeting, the woman, perhaps just a few years older than Emma's twenty-five years, paused. It only took a second before her eyes brightened. "Oh, wait! You're from the tree place, right? I'm so glad you were able to come after all. I thought they didn't have anyone available until tomorrow."

Not sure what to say, Emma pushed the door closed. Olive-green eyes blinked, a startling contrast to the woman's warm Creole skin. She seemed to be waiting for some kind of recognition or reaction from Emma. "You are here about the live oaks, aren't you?"

The woman sounded so sure of herself, Emma almost nodded out of reflex. Emma very well could have been, given that plants were her thing. "Not technically." She pushed a lock of hair behind her ear. "But if you're having trouble with your *quercus virginiana*, I could take a quick peek to make sure it isn't serious. Without looking, I'd guess it's probably wilt disease or leaf blister, but we need to make sure because if we're talking two-hundred-plus-year-old trees lining a drive somewhere—"

Emma was about to say how catastrophic it would be to lose even one of those irreplaceable trees, but the stricken look on the receptionist's face as she chewed on her bottom lip stopped Emma from listing dire consequences. To lose the centuries-old trees characteristic of antebellum plantations would be more of a financial blow than a historic attraction like this could overcome. Especially this one, it appeared.

Pausing as if time would erase her nerdy horticulturist outburst, Emma shrugged. "Actually, I'm here to see if you do tours." She surveyed the room for a sign with prices or times. "And although I'm not the botanist you must have called, I do know a little about plants. I could take a look while I'm here, if you like."

Emma wasn't sure why she was downplaying her skills, and was just about to say something about her degree in landscape architecture when the door behind her scraped jarringly across the wood floor. Both she and the receptionist turned their attention to the door. A young couple strode in, hand in hand, laughing about something that must have happened outside. They stepped to the counter, all grins and exuding sunshine and love.

"We're Grae and Tate." The young woman had a friendly smile and confident way. The kind of person Emma could be friends with. "We should be on the list for the tour?"

"Oh, yes." The receptionist consulted a heavy analog watch hung on a black velvet ribbon around her neck, and swallowed. She appeared anxious, probably because it was already five minutes past the hour. "The tour guide should arrive shortly. It looks like it will just be the three of you."

She looked at the young couple, then back to Emma. "It's twenty dollars each for the tour, and it takes roughly an hour. Unless Mr. Lambert ends up filling in. Knowing him, it could be a much longer tour once he gets to talking." She began collecting admissions from her customers. "I believe in fair warnings for all," she said with a sage nod. A set of small metal wind chimes tinkled near the door, but no breeze had blown through the room. "Mr. Lambert is here."

It was several full seconds before Emma could understand how the woman knew Mr. Lambert had arrived.

"You are late. Again!" Emma heard a man yelling from outside the office. There were more words she couldn't distinguish from both sides of the argument, not that she was trying. The words were terse, their tones rough. "You're done!" the man with authority—Mr. Lambert, Emma had to assume—said finally.

He wasn't yelling uncontrollably, but he was firm. And loud. Emma felt her chest tighten, as if she had to pull on thick skin to keep herself safe from this man.

The door opened one more time, and in walked Emma's savior from Live Oak Lane. Startled to see him in this setting and after the unwanted jolt of the overheard conversation, she watched as he wrenched the door open, clearly frustrated. Though she was sure he was the same man, he'd changed into comfortable-looking jeans and a plaid short-sleeved button-up.

"One more thing to add to the list, Zoe," he grumbled, and thumbed over his shoulder at the door.

"It's already there, Mr. Lambert." Zoe's voice held more than a hint of humor in it, and Emma found she preferred the woman's way of dealing with problems with a smile rather than the grump's irritation. Intrigued about the mysterious Mr. Lambert, Emma scrutinized Zoe's reaction to him. The receptionist didn't look the slightest bit alarmed, worried, or even reserved.

"Of course, if I knew my way around a toolbox, that list wouldn't be getting so unwieldy."

"We'll get it done, boss. No worries." Zoe tugged on the other necklace she wore, some sort of small fabric bag hung on a leather cord. A gris-gris, Emma had learned at a touristy voodoo shop in New Orleans.

"Yeah." Mr. Lambert's growl was like the rumble of a summer thunderstorm, low and quiet but with a barely reined-in forcefulness. "Especially if you keep using that voodoo magic on me."

It was confusing. The man had been explosively angry a moment before, but had cooled as he'd stepped inside. The playful way Zoe referred to him as her boss and his reaction almost hinted at flirtatiousness, though it seemed more comfortable than that. Old friends, perhaps.

Mr. Lambert turned a brooding look to those around

him, taking a moment to size up each member of the party. Emma felt the urge to examine her clothing, expecting to find bits of dirt or dried leaves clinging to her clothes from earlier. When his eyes fell on her, Emma thought she detected a glimmer of recognition, and she smiled, but his steady gaze was distressing.

Instead, he turned back to Zoe. "You're not taking money from these people, are you, Zoe?" He shook his head. "The place is hardly worth a frog leg and a hush-puppy in this condition, but a year from now . . . well, that'll be another story."

Zoe started to pull cash from the till, but Tate held up a palm to refuse. "Keep ours, if you don't mind. We're happy to pay, help with the needed repairs. We knew what we were getting into before we came."

Emma also waved Zoe off with her hand. "Add mine to the renovation fund as well."

"We don't need your charity donations," Mr. Lambert said. "We're not as poor as that."

If the man bristled at admissions, maybe the place really wasn't worth seeing. Had her great-grandfather's journal not led her here, she probably wouldn't stay.

Emma couldn't figure out what to make of Mr. Lambert. First of all, this whole "Mr. Lambert" thing was getting old. She had to find out his first name, because it was nuts thinking of someone as *mister* anything when he was roughly her age. At Live Oak

Lane he'd been more than pleasant, flirty even. However, hearing him fire an employee made her uncomfortable. And even though she thought they'd shared a moment after he'd rescued her chair, now he didn't even seem to remember her. It left her uncertain and on edge, but at least he seemed pleasant enough with everyone, other than the employee—*ex-employee*. And the door, which he yanked open.

He looked over his shoulder to Zoe. "We better move this repair to the top of the list." Mr. Lambert turned back to the group, holding the door open. "If everyone will follow me into the parking lot. Ladies..."

As the guests filed through, Emma's interest piqued. Was the true Mr. Lambert the nice guy or the beast others seemed to think he was? Though she decided to be cautious around him, Emma would give Mr. Lambert the benefit of the doubt. He'd been kind to her, and though clearly upset, he hadn't taken it out on Zoe, or anyone else for that matter. That was enough for now.

"Despite what Zoe called me, I'm Theo," he said once he rounded the group into a small circle in the parking lot. "If you'll follow in your cars, we'll take a short drive over to the main property and go from there."

His battered pickup led them through yet another gate at the back of the lot. When she rounded the corner, Emma caught her breath with a start. In contrast to Live Oak Lane's impeccably manicured trees, Indigo Pointe's double line of ancient oaks felt wild and free, more natural than the staged Live Oak Lane. Thick trees with gnarled, twisting branches blocked the sun, veiling the air with an eerie undertow. Emma could see it in the shadows, feel it in the humidity. Ghosts of the past reached forward like a tangled vine.

A shiver ran down her spine as her eyes followed the allée to a double row of simple wooden structures that had to have been slave cabins. There were too many of them, placed too symmetrically, each exactly like the next. The gravity of it hit her as no other plantation on her trip had, making the air difficult to breathe.

Even in the gloom—or perhaps because of it—the scene was overwhelmingly, achingly beautiful in its natural, historic feel. Theo led their train of vehicles into a small gravel pullout and Emma rushed to park. She stepped from the car, taking a deep breath and allowing the quietness to settle into her. She'd stepped into a dichotomous fairy-tale land of good and evil, wealth and poverty, hope and disillusionment.

While the others slowly climbed out of their cars, Emma pulled out a camera and headed toward the trees, staying just far enough back to capture the three-foot picket fence of decaying wood at the head of the allée. She snapped a couple of photos of the lichen growing on the boards and the resurrection ferns in the V of the trees.

Many of the oak leaves were edged in brown—something that didn't usually happen until they were shed from the tree every March. She stepped closer, verifying her suspicion of leaf blister. While the disease looked alarming with its misshapen and prematurely browning leaves, it was fairly benign. She reached out to examine the closest branch. Several leaves were cupped and twisted, thicker and tougher than a healthy, leathery leaf. Several were infected with a fuzzy ball about the size of a BB on the backside. She bent over and picked up a couple of the grounded leaves. For the most part, they looked normal. A couple of different issues were at play, but with the proper care, the trees would remain healthy.

"If you'll all gather over here," Theo called her back to them, waiting until she rejoined them before continuing. "We'll take a tour of the gardens behind the house before we go inside. But don't worry, you will get your chance to take all the pictures you want." He rolled his eyes, and she felt the sting.

As if all she wanted were some lame pictures. She'd only meant to help. Saving the trees would mean so much more to her than some photo that would end up buried in her computer files.

To their right, a split-rail fence edged a pen of various grazing farm animals. To the left were several buildings arranged in a square around an elaborate garden with the main house at the far end. With Grae and Tate wrapped up in each other, Emma found herself walking in step with Theo, but riveted by the scene around her. Perhaps not so much with the garden's originality, but with its potential.

Theo went through his spiel about the Greek Revival style of the home and garden, but Emma's trained eye snagged on the exceptions, instances where the cultivation and care of the garden had altered the plan over the past century and a half. The maze of shrubbery came almost to Emma's shoulders and needed a good trim to look uniform and healthy and to encourage new growth between the individual plants. The brick pavers were in decent shape, but a few were cracked or displaced and could be attended to with little effort.

Overall, the property had a wildness about it that mirrored the man walking next to her. An overgrown, untamed feeling she felt emanating from both. Yet it was exactly those qualities that enchanted her like none of the others had.

CHAPTER 3

As the tiny group headed toward the gardens, Theo couldn't help but notice everything about the beautiful brunette who walked alongside him. Her petite frame made him feel like a giant, yet she didn't seem to notice. Occasionally, he caught the light floral scent from when he'd met her earlier, and every once in a while, he heard a few stray notes of a song she hummed that he almost recognized. If he could just get enough notes in a row . . .

It had been a long time since someone had caught his attention as she did, but Theo needed to pull his thoughts together if he wanted to make a good impression. Having owned the plantation a few short weeks, he'd been on the tour only twice to familiarize himself with the process, but he hadn't yet run one himself. Of course, there would have to be an enchanting distraction his first time through.

She was beautiful for sure, as well as perceptive and observant. She walked confidently, noticing everything as her eyes and camera paused on things that made him wish, more than ever, that the place was up to his usual standards. Fascinated, Theo watched as she gracefully rose on tiptoes to angle her camera through the branches of one of the younger trees.

What must she see through that camera lens? If only he'd taken the time to pull out the garden shears rather than taking over the tour, but somebody had to do it. That so-called history major from whichever of the zillion New Orleans area universities wasn't worth the paper his résumé was written on. Not only was he perpetually late and hung over if his bloodshot eyes were any indication, but Don didn't know what he was talking about, which was inexcusable. To Theo, things like accuracy of historical details on the plantation tour were more than niceties; they were essentials.

The couple for this morning's tour had signed up online, and Theo had been loath to cancel on out-of-towners even with the property in its disappointing condition. Indigo Pointe had been running tours for the better part of thirty years, and Theo wouldn't interrupt the market flow, no matter how slow the trickle. It would be easier to increase a weak dribble than start over after completely stopping it. Advertising had been altogether too weak, but he wouldn't push that until the place was in much more marketable shape. He'd been so focused on acquiring the property for nostalgic reasons, he hadn't worried much about business viability. Hopefully it wouldn't be a decision he wound up regretting.

How surprised he'd been when he walked into the office and found the beautiful woman he'd encountered at Live Oak Lane that morning. He hadn't been sure how to address the situation after his embarrassment over firing Don, which she had to have overheard. Once again, he'd let his explosive temper get the better of him. All he could think to do was to pretend he didn't recognize her, though any red-blooded man wouldn't have bought it.

The woman wasn't exactly forgettable. She was beautiful in a classic sense, with thick, long hair so dark it was only one shade away from black. Her huge, almond-shaped eyes were a deep brown with something else—a little green, perhaps, or even copper? He'd have to get a better look.

He led the tour down a dirt path beyond the pair of late-nineteenth-century barns toward the back of the main house and its parterre garden. The sun was out now that the rain had stopped, which added to the vibrant greens of the plants but surely encouraged more weed growth even as they spoke. The air was temperate despite the early summer date. He'd take a mild June day while he could, especially if he got to spend a few of these hours with a woman who reminded him there was more to life than work.

He swept his arm around him, pointing out each of the matching structures set symmetrically around the garden, as he spoke. "The original owner, an immigrant from Germany, started with a traditional Creole home, quite a bit more modest than what you see here. Two generations later, the grandson who inherited the property decided to improve his image by remodeling his ancestral home in the Greek Revival style. That was when the gardens and additional buildings were added. In accordance with the style, each building has its mirror image across the garden square, with the exception of the big house."

He turned to face the much smaller building opposite the main house. It took center stage a short walk from the mansion through the garden. "Any guesses what this structure might be?"

He liked this part of the tour, and although he'd heard that many guests guessed correctly, there were sometimes some humorous suggestions.

"Some sort of Grecian temple?"

Did the woman ever let go of her guy's hand? They were at that cute stage of their relationship. Not for the first time, Theo felt a slight pang of jealousy. He hadn't experienced a relationship like that in quite a while, and being confronted with it now made him realize how much he missed sharing his life with someone special.

"But," Grae refuted her own prediction, "I'm guessing *that* building" —she pointed over at the small church on the east side of the property— "is where they worshipped." She didn't seem to have a real theory of the purpose of the miniature building.

"I'm going with outhouse," her boyfriend suggested.

"You got it," Theo said to the man, not allowing himself to be disappointed. It probably took a kid to come up with something creative.

By that time they'd walked to the center of the garden, where a bronze cherub held a sundial burnished with a beautiful patina. Theo slowed, allowing the patrons to wander through the chest-high, maze-like hedges that were easily the home's best feature.

"Will we get a chance to go inside and upstairs?" the pretty woman asked, her eyes big behind stylish frames.

Theo had never been so attracted to someone who gave off the nerd vibe before. Luckily, she didn't seem to notice his stare as she took in the two-story main house from the back. He didn't follow her gaze, choosing instead to look at her.

"I'd love to see the overall composition of the garden from above," she said. "I bet it's breathtaking."

Breathtaking. That she was.

But if she thought the gardens at Indigo Pointe were good, she must have never seen any of the iconic European ones. The English, French, Italian, and Greeks all boasted much more impressive offerings than this modest piece of land in Louisiana. While it was nothing compared to his other holdings sprinkled around the world, when he'd heard of this opportunity to collect the last piece of his family's puzzle, Theo didn't even need to think twice. To purchase the last holdout of the Indigo Pointe Plantation, the plot that included the historic buildings, had been on his bucket list since he started in real estate.

"Of course, Miss . . ." He loved being able to use Southern manners to get beautiful women's names.

"Emma." She stuck out her hand to shake, and he grasped her hand lightly, noticing rough calluses on her hand. He gave a slight squeeze as she followed up with "Emma Treager."

He dropped her hand. Treager. The name that was spat like a swear word in his home growing up. *Treagers*, his grandmother had said anytime they'd come to Indigo Pointe. *Never trust them, Theo. Someday they'll come slinking around, ready to steal back everything, you mark my word!*

His heart jumped into overdrive. Was that why she was here?

She looked innocent enough, and if she could play it cool, so could he, but that didn't mean he wouldn't keep an eye on her.

"Yes, I'll make sure you get a chance to see the gardens from above, Miss Emma Treager," he spoke softly just to her, but then turned to include the lovesick couple who lagged behind. "Over here to our left is the detached kitchen."

He walked them through one set of double doors and then opened the other to demonstrate how the cook would attempt to diffuse the stifling heat from the huge fireplace and brick oven. Other than a sink and a couple of large tables, the room didn't hold much else. Theo explained how the building would have been used and who would have worked here. After fielding a few questions, mostly from the lovely and suspicious Emma, he took the group outside again, winding them along brick paths, explaining the purposes of the other small buildings that flanked the courtyard.

Other than the main house and kitchen, none of the other buildings were open on the tour. The two garçonnières had been modernized, one of which was his home away from home when he didn't want to drive to his home in the French Quarter. The other bachelor cottage, situated next to the outdoor kitchen, was where a caretaker could live as soon as he hired one.

Other buildings on the property were way too run-down for tourists. The church that Grae had pointed out would be an asset to the tour, but there was no way he could let anyone inside. After an old fire who knows how long ago followed by a badly botched remodel only half a century ago, subsequent decades of neglect had it on the cusp of crumbling. The one gothic rose window that survived was worth renovating the building for. The colors of the stained glass were subtle at the moment, but when backlit by the morning light through the building, it was phenomenal.

Theo felt lucky that the core buildings at least had been maintained enough to keep them from falling into complete ruins. The place was an embarrassment. He was flabbergasted that it had passed safety inspections and wondered if it was truly safe for the public. Overall, it made him feel itchy, like wearing wet wool on a hot day. He was used to the things around him being impeccable, stylish, and tasteful; right now the place said lazy, backward, and slow. But it wouldn't always; he would turn things around.

About to explain how the pigeonniers were little more than status symbols housing pigeons for family dinners, Theo turned to face his entourage only to realize Emma was no longer with them. He paused in his speech, twirling on his heel to find her in the shadow of the church, her hands in the soil under one of the rosebushes.

A flash of anger swelled. Of all the things the woman could get into, why was she meddling with the one he cared most about? This rare variant had always been a favorite of his mother's. On the verge of dying, its once champagne-colored blossoms now looked almost colorless, and if she killed it by messing around, he'd sue.

"Miss Emma?" He growled loudly to be heard over the distance.

She looked up from her crouched position, allowing the dirt to sift through her fingers in clumps, and then stood, brushing her hands together. "You can drop the 'Miss.' Plain Emma is just fine."

She was anything but plain, even with the smudge of mud on her wrists and her hair getting caught on the rose thorns, but he had very little tolerance for meddlers. "Okay, ma'am." Satisfaction swelled in his chest at the scowl crossing her delicate features. He'd known ma'am would be worse than calling her miss. "The tour does not include tampering with the plants. Stick with the group, if you don't mind."

She walked toward the group, still clapping her hands together, but there was no way the dirt was going to come off without soap and water. As far as he knew, the water in the cookhouse where they'd just been wasn't functional, but his eyes halted on a small bucket at the corner of the house. It probably had collected rainwater over the past couple of days.

"There's a bucket, if you'd like to wash." The offering was almost an insult, and his voice was too gruff, but she responded with a smile. His heart skipped again. This was crazy. How could she be so frustrating and so intriguing at the same time?

While she washed, Theo tapped out a quick text to Zoe. *See what you can find out about Emma Treager.*

Will do, boss. If she's the one on your tour, she told me she knows about plants. Is that what you're looking for?

Hmm. That made sense. *And anything else, including the Treager part.* That should be enough for Zoe to get what he was asking.

Theo led them around to the front lawn, where they could take in the mansion's true grandeur for the first time. It was rather odd to do this back-door tour when a gorgeous wrought iron gate stood covered up at the street. One of his main goals was to improve the grounds with a suitable grand entrance, throw open the gate, and welcome visitors the proper way.

While his family's connection with the plantation was a complex one, Theo had been reared to covet the place. Indigo Pointe was the one that got away, the one always just out of the Lamberts' grasp, and Theo had finally attained it. He bought it, not necessarily to add to his collection of homes, but rather to preserve his family heritage. Keeping it open to the public was an additional obligation and passion of his as well. As problematic as the history was, antebellum tourist sites played a key role in achieving civil rights and racial reconciliation. While it might be more comfortable to allow reminders of slavery to quietly crumble away, reclaimed by time, all history needed to be preserved, even if it was painful. Especially if it was painful.

The ironic part was that when the community at large discovered he was the owner, they assumed he was a descendant of slave owners, and therefore worthy of their disrespect. That was probably what rankled him the most: people making assumptions about him and his family.

"Watch your step," he called out as his guests trekked across the spotty grass to capture the entire building in one camera shot. This was exactly why he needed to add a driveway of some sort—so women's heels didn't sink into the Louisiana mud and come back dragging a crawdad or two.

In front of them, the house rose, its pedimented portico in the center anchoring two semi-circular staircases to the upper, main floor. Around the front and sides were twelve massive Doric columns, so thick he didn't think two people could hold hands around the base.

The four of them traipsed up the concrete and metal

stairs, which were in decent repair but still held the overall wear of time. Theo found himself taking inventory, the ever-expanding punch list for Zoe growing like a weed.

"The big house was originally built in the late 1790s and remodeled less than forty years later in the early 1830s." He'd already told them some of this, but had left out crucial details. His eyes drifted to Emma, and he found himself struggling to get back on script. The woman was confusing. If she was there as a Treager, checking up on Indigo Pointe, why was she so focused on the plants? It made no sense. "The staircases and columns were added at that time. I find it interesting that the columns are actually plastered brick."

"Brick?" Tate didn't sound like he believed Theo, but led right into what Theo had wanted to say about them, so he smiled.

"Yes, pie-shaped bricks. We have one of the original molds back at the office museum, if you want to take a look. Placed in a circle, the wedge bricks were then covered in a coat of thick lime with a lime wash over top."

While he loved history, this tour guide gig was never supposed to be his job. Two days ago, he wouldn't have been the one pointing out the bow tie pieces of wood that held together the pine planks, or the Haint blue ceilings on the gallery porch to ward off evil spirits. He tried not to care that his firing Don would surely get back to the kid's university history department, adding to his beastly reputation. Fine. There were plenty of other universities in the New Orleans area; surely someone would want a job running tours.

Theo racked his brain to remember what came next. He'd studied it over the past couple of weeks so he would be prepared just in case, and eventually that Oxford education of his had to amount for something, didn't it? It would be easier, perhaps, if Emma hadn't already sidetracked him with insightful questions about the structures and the history. At the same time, she seemed much more interested in the plants and grounds. Her motives were baffling, and she left his head spinning.

"When the owner remodeled the exterior of the home, it was all in an attempt to make the plantation look more prosperous and the family more prestigious than they actually were—an ironic facade covering up the truth. The family, and the plantation, never fully recovered from the investment, and it led to their . . . eventual . . . financial ruin about a century later."

He found himself struggling, not over the content this time, but in anticipation of Emma's reaction about her family history. But she didn't even seem to be listening. Maybe she *wasn't* checking up on him. Maybe she didn't know.

He should quit stressing himself out second-guessing her motives and take the opportunity fate had given him. If he hadn't been doing this tour, he never would have run into Emma again after this morning. There had to be some way he could get her number, ask her out, some way to make sure he would see her again. If she was checking up on him, he wanted to know why. If she wasn't, he wanted to know *her*.

"As we go inside," he said, opening the side doors into one of the second story's three main rooms, "I must insist that photography of the interior is completely off limits. It's one of the few requests we make here at Indigo Pointe."

Emma looked crestfallen and swung the camera strap over her neck, a complicit acquiescence. She stepped through, pausing to lift a hand to the eighteen-inch-thick brick stuccoed walls. The woman noticed everything. Was she making a list for a lawsuit? Inventorying what she believed was somehow rightfully hers?

Theo almost felt bad about not allowing photography, but he had his reasons. And he allowed so much other freedom. He couldn't think of many historical sites that allowed tourists access to almost every room in the house without pushing them through a cordoned-off cattle chute. Not that there was much to see. The rooms, while technically furnished in antique period pieces, were dark and small. The paintings were dull. Whether caked with dirt and dust, or the result of faded paints, he was tempted to replace them.

He led the group quickly through the room into a better-lit hallway at the back of the house. Here sunlight streamed through plentiful windows, the light bouncing off of the gleaming hardwood floors. "Feel free to photograph the back gardens through the upstairs window." There was Emma's smile that he'd been hoping for, making his concession worth every ounce of control it cost him.

"Wait." Grae stopped, looking around her as if she missed something. "That's it? One room deep?"

Theo appreciated both Grae's observation and Emma's enthusiastic reaction. Already at the window, Emma didn't hesitate to start snapping pictures of the garden. From this vantage point, the design of the hedges was striking.

He turned to Grae. "That's something about this house that surprises many. With its grandiose front, the mansion gives the impression that it is massive, when really it is just one room deep and three rooms across. You'd never guess from the outside, would you?"

Grae and Tate shook their heads.

Emma had turned her sharp eye from admiring the view to scanning the room, seeming to try to memorize everything, paying particular attention to the paintings, the books on the shelves, and even papers lying on the desk. It was almost as if she were looking for something specific. A flutter of unease hit his stomach, but he pushed it away. The place was legally his, and she couldn't do anything about it, even if her last name was Treager.

"This hallway used to be the back porch." Theo ignored Emma, a challenge for him at the moment, to continue with the tour. "Which was often used as a sleeping porch as well. With no center hallway between the home's rooms, the only way to go from one to the other was by stepping through the doors at the front or rear of the room and out onto one of the porches. Opening both sides was their early air conditioning system."

This time, when his eyes flicked back to Emma as they always did, he found her with camera in hand, finger working the shutter. Was she actually taking a snapshot of a doorknob and the swinging lock cover over its keyhole? Annoyance surged again. He'd had *one* rule. Was she hard of hearing, forgetful, or merely feeling entitled?

Just when he thought he liked her.

Theo stalked up behind Emma and whispered over her shoulder, barely able to restrain his frustration. "I have asked—" He felt a cruel satisfaction when she jumped. "And quite nicely, I might add, that you refrain from interior photography."

She turned to face him, her hands shaking. As they should be. Why should she break the rules? She was a guest in someone else's house. His.

"Sorry." She put the camera and her trembling hands, behind her back and stepped away, joining Grae and Tate at a bank of portraits.

With a sliver of guilt at his outburst, he let Emma pass by. He took a step closer to the door to examine for himself what she'd been photographing. He'd always assumed all of the rooms in the house had the same antique brass fittings. They were ornate compared to today's standards, but little more than rectangles with fluting and keyhole covers shaped like tassels.

Emma had found an exception. Four ivy leaves spiraled around the doorknob, with more along the sides of the knob plate, hinges, and striker plate. The most unique part was the leaf-shaped keyhole cover.

The coloring and shapes of the two patterns were so similar, they tended to blend together. Why had they stood out to Emma? It was, after all, just a doorknob.

Emma, Grae, and Tate were examining the portraits, pointing out family traits like wide, almond-shaped eyes and an intellectual air, when Theo stepped over to join them. He wanted to smooth things over but wasn't sure how, especially since his gut told him he needed to get her to erase the photos.

"So has this always been a family-owned plantation, then?" Emma asked, startling him this time. She really didn't know?

She seemed unaware there was blood between them. Bad blood. While his family and hers weren't exactly related, their histories were entwined in the largest real-life feud he'd ever heard of.

"Not exactly. Indigo Pointe was established by one of the families who settled what later became known as the German Coast. In fact, the next plantation over" — Theo pointed east to where his family's plantation had once stood— "was settled by a good family friend around the same time. Eventually the two families had a bit of a falling out because one opposed slaveholding while the other was swept along with the status quo."

A bit of a falling out was understating it. They hated each other, as far as he knew.

"Was it possible for a plantation owner to oppose slaveholding at the time?" Emma seemed surprised, yet pleased by the idea. "Wasn't that the key to making any kind of profit?"

Theo tugged at his collar, wishing he'd brought along a bottle of water. Getting into sticky family history wasn't what he'd planned, and he needed to find a way out as smoothly as possible.

"Holding slaves really was the only way for a plantation to get ahead financially, which was probably why the owners here did it. The family I mentioned that didn't have slaves" —*his*, he neglected to add— "didn't end up faring well at the time. They were barely able to keep their family fed. They never had the funds to expand until well after the War and plantation economics changed."

That was also the beginning of the end of the Treager family's reign at Indigo Pointe.

Purposely omitting the founding owner's surname made his speech less official-sounding, but then he wasn't about to mention Emeric Treager. If Emma didn't already know she had the last name of Indigo Pointe's one-time owners, he didn't want to tell her.

"After renovations were made to the house and gardens, the plantation fell on hard times. To stay afloat, the family tried switching crops. They started with indigo and rice, and then, more than a century ago, switched to sugarcane. Even that, however, didn't end their financial woes, and eventually they started selling off parcels of land, usually to the family next door, who helped them keep the plantation running. Then, during the Great Depression, the family had to sell the remaining plot—including all the buildings and gardens. So while this has been a working plantation for over two centuries, and still is, it has not been in the same family the entire time."

"Did they sell the house to that family, then?"

Theo had hoped she wouldn't ask. Family grudges, passed down like his blue eyes and love of adventure, reared up inside his chest. "They did not."

He swallowed the bile at the back of his throat and tried to remain professional. All's well that ended well, right? And the fact of the matter was that a century after the slight, the plantation was owned by that family now. Indigo Pointe belonged, in its entirety, to the Lambert family.

CHAPTER 4

What was this guy's deal? Emma couldn't think of anything less innocuous than taking a picture of a doorknob, for Pete's sake. She'd known Theo was upset, but he'd been keeping it together, mostly, until, like a twig snapping in two, he got all bent out of shape over something as stupid as a picture. Really?

Goosebumps erupted down both of her arms when the infernal man came to stand next to her, pretending to look at the family photos. She couldn't concentrate on them with him standing next to her, not with his tempting scent of aftershave of evergreen bushes and something else she couldn't place. Not when she was mad at him.

Emma crossed the narrow hallway and stood in

front of a framed pedigree of the property, a list of the plantation's owners, but the adrenaline from the previous confrontation kept her from being able to focus.

This time she heard his footsteps coming up behind her. She stiffened her back and held her jaw tight. She wasn't going to let him catch her off guard again.

"Delete it." The words were a fiery blast into her ear.

"Why?" She raised one hand, flicking her wrist as she challenged, though she didn't turn to look at him. It was a ridiculous rule.

"That was the condition I placed from the start. I don't have to explain myself to you."

There was no answering that one. Although she didn't agree with the rule—thought it was dumb, honestly—that didn't mean she was justified in ignoring it.

Emma could feel Theo's body heat just inches behind her. It was both agonizing and exhilarating.

The silence became a battle, one she was determined to win. Theo couldn't force her to delete the photo, and he certainly couldn't make her talk.

Tate cleared his throat behind them, and both Emma and Theo turned toward the couple, the interruption welcome for Emma at least.

"We're going to head back outside. Grae wanted to

look at the sundial again, see how accurate it is now that it's been a good hour." Tate checked his phone, presumably for the time. Emma felt for him. She hadn't meant to make the couple uncomfortable, just . . . him.

"No problem," Theo said, as calm and friendly as ever. "We'll meet you out there in a minute."

At least his voice no longer held the threatening tone, but of course he was speaking to Tate, who'd done nothing wrong. She had been the one to tick Theo off.

She'd set him off, but he was already so near the edge, it hadn't been hard. The question was how to deal with him now. Emma wouldn't cower, if that was what he wanted. She wouldn't give up just because he showed a little verbal muscle. If he wanted to engage, she could be a formidable opponent, but was going toe to toe with Theo the best way to get the information she needed? So far, she'd learned the most when he wasn't paying attention to her.

Theo had done well filling in as tour guide on the fly. Even after hearing almost the same speech at every plantation, she had learned something in his tour: pie-shaped bricks.

And the German Coast. Another piece of her family puzzle, she was sure. Her great-grandfather's description of a plantation with curving staircases had led her here, and finding the ivy pattern convinced her she was in the right place. Now she had to be on the lookout for

Opa's family treasure—the problem was that she had no idea what kind of treasure it was. Emma had carefully examined everything from the books and papers on the desk to the antique furniture around the room, but nothing seemed all that remarkable.

With her luck, it was probably some ugly, old painting, since she wouldn't know a valuable one if there was a neon sign pointing straight at it. Maybe she should just ask the stuffy "Mr. Lambert" if he had any idea about this, but there was no way he'd tell her if it actually was valuable.

The ivy detail, though, had caught her attention immediately. In an area of the country where the fleur-de-lis was dominant, the ivy design was out of place and too unique to be a coincidence.

Her heart thumped with the knowledge that she was on the right path. Already she had photographs of the curved staircases and the maze-like garden Opa reminisced about. She'd even tied the box to the plantation. If she could uncover its history and find the treasure, she'd be set. Though that was quite the *if*. But even if she got no more, with these photographs, Emma could help Opa anchor his shadowy memories, wisps of stories told to him by his own father and grandfather. She could gift him peace.

Emma had always been intrigued by that mahogany box in Opa's library. Square-based but angled in front, it was like a miniature secretary desk with a similar purpose. Tiny square compartments held inkwells, long since spent and dried but still just as glorious with their tiny brass lids that screwed on and off. Long, skinny nooks were perfect for holding quills or pens. Various-sized slots were perfect for today's business cards, note cards, and paper clips.

A leather blotter was tucked into the bottom of the box. Hinged at the middle, it could be opened to provide a smooth writing pad and had obviously been well used over the decades, as it boasted an ink stain or two from a leaky fountain pen.

The box held history, a feeling of tradition and permanence, memories sitting next to Opa, learning to write her name with his calligraphy pen. Several of her ancestors must have penned love letters and business correspondence on it; perhaps even her great-grandfather had written this very journal on the pull-out shelf. If she could inherit just one thing, she would choose that box, especially as she learned more about its history and this special place it was tied to.

With the official tour all but concluded, unless Emma could come up with something, her sleuthing days were over. She'd have no valid excuse to hang around the plantation looking for more.

Disappointment filled her feet with lead. She couldn't leave Indigo Pointe without searching the place top to bottom for more information about the Treagers. Her only choice was to trust Theo. Perhaps if she explained what she was up to, he might be interested enough to help her search.

Her imagination conjured up a variety of potential reactions to her telling him why she was there—maybe Theo would yell for her to get out. He might tell her she had no right to be there, but she could handle that. What she wouldn't do was leave without even trying. She'd seen slivers of good in the man that day, and she decided to hope that was who he truly was inside.

At the sound of a text chime, Theo checked his phone, and by the time he put it away again, Emma had made her decision.

"Can I show you something?"

Theo looked skeptical, but nodded.

Emma pulled the leather-bound journal from her bag. On the plane ride from Boise to New Orleans, she'd tagged a couple of the yellowed pages with sticky notes, marking the few key clues she had in this family mystery.

She flipped to a page about three-quarters of the way through and turned it around so Theo could see. She'd studied the sketch so long it often found its way into her dreams. She knew without double-checking that it matched the ivy pattern perfectly.

Emma caught a change in Theo's expression and

realized he'd made the connection between the box's ivy-shaped lock cover in the sketch and the matching one on the door in the house. The pattern was so distinct, they had to have been crafted by the same artist. Theo's lake-blue eyes looked up from the journal's pages, and he cocked an eyebrow at her.

He patted the journal with the palm of a large hand. "What is this?" At least he sounded more curious than anything.

"I'm trying to unravel a mystery."

Both of his eyebrows went up this time in unasked question.

She wondered how much she wanted to share. She carefully took the book from Theo's hands. "It's my great-grandfather's journal, and I have a feeling *that* lock" —she pointed back at the door— "is a huge piece in the family puzzle I'm here to solve."

"And what is this family puzzle?" Was that suspicion that touched his words with frost?

Of course he'd ask, but she was hesitant to explain the treasure hunt she was on. Not only would it sound silly to say it out loud, but she didn't trust him. The place was his, so the treasure would be also, and although she wouldn't steal from him, she at least wanted to unravel the mystery.

"Opa wants to know the history of this box, and I'm

trying to find out for his upcoming hundredth birthday party."

"Hmm." Theo stood both several inches taller and wider than she, making her feel small and vulnerable, but his expression was soft, intrigued, as he seemed to consider. "Okay, Emma Treager, you may keep your photographs on two conditions. First, promise me this photo will not end up online. I'll know where it came from if it does." He left the unspoken threat hanging in the air until she nodded. She could live with that.

A smirk transformed his handsome face into stone. "Second, you earn it. You work for me."

CHAPTER 5

In Theo's estimation, the shock on Emma's face was priceless. That must have come out of nowhere for her, which made it all the better. Little did she know he'd vetted her through Zoe, finding out enough of Emma's background to know he needed her skills. The photo was just a good excuse.

"Should we head outside?" While Theo liked the idea of spending time alone with Emma, he didn't want to force an answer from her. He was smart enough to know she would probably turn him down. With the way he'd lost his temper over the photographs, it could only end badly. Allowing time to settle between them, to provide more opportunities to see the real him rather than the jumpy, defensive man she'd just witnessed, would only help his case. "I should probably see if Tate and Grae have any more questions, thank them . . . you know, be a good tour guide."

He wasn't sure what her look was supposed to mean, and wished he had the ability to read her mind. He led the way down the back wooden staircase and out the rear door of the manor. Generally, he was fairly good at figuring out what women thought about him, but then, his relationship track record wasn't that great. He wouldn't dwell on it. Things were going to change this time. He'd make sure of it. If he was honest with himself, he was attracted to Emma, and not only physically; he liked that she didn't care what others thought when she fiddled around in the dirt on a tour or took furtive photographs.

On the other hand, he'd pretty much given the poor woman an ultimatum. That wasn't going to help his string of failed relationships. Maybe he needed to pull out *How to Win Friends and Influence People* again, because he was fairly certain this particular tactic wasn't hidden in any of those chapters—even between the lines.

He'd been mostly kidding about Emma working for him, but with the text he'd received from Zoe, the one touting Emma's newly minted master's degree in landscape architecture, meeting her was serendipity. He could tell he needed to hire Emma with every step they took back toward their vehicles because she stopped occasionally to touch a leaf, wave a fragrance toward her nose, check the dampness of the soil. Anything relating to gardening was way out of his element, but she seemed to be a master.

"I was serious about the job offer, Emma." Theo stopped in the church rose garden, far enough away that Tate and Grae, who were taking pictures in the live oaks, couldn't overhear. He instinctively reached out to touch the velvety petal of one of the reds, which dropped off the bloom like it was weighted. Should it be doing that? He shoved his hands into his pockets. "I know better than anyone the landscaping needs work."

"You have no idea." She almost smirked at him.

She was right, of course. What did he know of the plantation? He'd only officially owned the place for a few weeks. Not only was he completely bereft of any horticultural knowledge—it had been part of the plan to hire someone to take care of that for him—but secrets about the property's past? The fact that there might be some captivated his imagination.

"At least I have an idea that I have no idea."

He had more than an idea, really. He had memories.

Long after the Treagers had sold the main house and the sugarcane fields were owned by the Lambert family, the owner from California arranged for them to keep an eye on the property. Although Theo had been to the plantation several times growing up, usually with his uncle, the plantation foreman, he'd never noticed anything out of the ordinary. Lambert family lore held that Indigo Pointe did indeed have a secret—a hidden treasure that his family felt was *theirs*, kept from them by the Treagers. That had been the source of the family feud, as far as Theo had gathered. It was a shame, really.

The families had come to America from the same village around the same time, and for generations, they'd helped each other navigate a new climate with new crops. Being on opposite ends of the slavery issue caused friction in the families' relationships; it was this treasure that severed it completely.

"I had Zoe do a quick reference check on you." Theo could see Emma getting ready to protest, and he stopped her. "When you kept fiddling with my plants, I had a right to know. With your degree and your love of history, I think Indigo Pointe could be a good fit." He paused. "That is, if you don't already have a position elsewhere." He wasn't used to even asking. Usually when people knew who he was, they were the ones angling for jobs. "And if you do, I'm sure I could offer a competitive salary."

"What is it you're looking for, Mr. Lambert?"

He cocked his head at her and raised his eyebrow. "Don't go all 'Mr. Lambert' on me. I already have Zoe doing that far too much."

Emma blew out a sigh. "Fine. What is it you want

from me, Theo?" She put way too much emphasis on the name.

"You want your ill-gotten photograph." He made sure to emphasize what she was getting out of the bargain. "And I need this place spiffed up *toute de suite*. Remember Live Oak Lane this morning?" Of course she would. That was all everyone thought of when it came to Louisiana plantations. "I want Indigo Pointe to be more iconic, more realistic, more photographed."

Zoe had also confirmed that Emma was a descendant of Emeric Treager, *the* Emeric Treager of Indigo Pointe, and if Emma didn't know of their family feud, she would as soon as she mentioned him to her parents. But he had the feeling that her desire to unravel this family mystery would ensure her acceptance of this little job offer. Part of him wondered if it was wise to invite someone who could be considered his foe into his territory, but he was less concerned with acquiring the value of the treasure and more concerned with finding it. Curiosity, at this point in his life, was way more of an incentive than money.

Was there more to this mystery than the metalwork of the doorknob matching that of the wooden box? Did she know about the treasure as well? It didn't make sense if she wasn't aware of her family's ties to Indigo. But why wouldn't she? It was easy enough to trace.

And if she didn't know before she got there, she

should have recognized her own name, right? While the first few generations of Indigo's owners were named Heidel, the surname Treager about halfway down the list should have caught her eye. Then again, he hadn't exactly given her much time in front of it.

If she hadn't figured it out already, he might as well tell her himself ... except that he didn't want to put a wedge between them. What if she held it against him that he owned what she thought should be hers?

"Are we talking a temporary job or long-term here?"

So she was considering it? Which did she want?

"That's negotiable. There's plenty of work to keep you busy for quite a while, but for now, I guess I was thinking of getting the most important things checked off as quickly as possible—in and done."

CHAPTER 6

Theo had done as much damage control as he could; now he needed to give Emma time to consider.

"We'd better head back—" Theo started, but Emma surprised him by cutting him off.

"Do you mind if I walk the grounds a little so I can see what I would be getting into?" Emma motioned a graceful hand toward the office.

As if he could trust her to go straight there. "Umm . . ." She wouldn't have time to get into anything, right? "Sure."

Theo looked toward the parking lot and noticed Grae and Tate climbing into their car. "See you back at the office, then?" Theo called over his shoulder to Emma as he broke into a jog toward the cars. He should at least try to be a good guide and thank the young couple for coming.

"I won't be far behind." Emma's words almost disappeared in the afternoon mist.

Theo tried to focus on the job at hand. He rushed over to Tate's side of the car to bid them farewell through the driver's side window, and then got into his own vehicle and followed them back to the office parking lot, where the two diverged. Waving goodbye, Theo parked his pickup and went in search for Zoe.

"I can't believe I did that." He found her in the kitchen behind the main office, scooping cookie dough onto a baking pan. "I offered her a job."

Not moving her head, Zoe raised her eyebrows to look at him. "And that's a problem why?"

"I don't know if I can work with her." He groaned. "She's headstrong and bossy."

Zoe rolled her eyes at him. "You mean she's a go-getter. And knowledgeable." She pulled a clean spoon from the drawer, scooped a bit of cookie dough, and handed it to him. "Be grateful. We've been trying to get someone out for the trees since you bought the place, and I'm not holding my breath that they'll show up tomorrow. You need Emma."

"What if she steals more from me?"

"More?" Zoe looked up and put her elbows on the kitchen bar, waiting for details.

He knew it was lame before he said it, and sighed. "I told them no photography inside the house and she had to challenge me on it."

"Ah, that's where you got the headstrong part. I was wondering." She went back to loading the baking pan. "You do know that's not really stealing."

"But I'd just said—"

Zoe lifted a hand and he stopped. "What do you think she's going to steal from you? If there was one scrap of something valuable, don't you think it would be long gone by now?"

"Antebellum antiques are worth plenty, but that's not what I'm talking about. She's here to find the Treager treasure."

Zoe scoffed. "That's just legend. It has to be. No one's found it in a century."

This wasn't the point. "It doesn't matter what it is. Everything on this property is mine, my family's."

"You don't need the money."

"Maybe not, but the Treagers have already taken enough. The treasure was supposed to belong to us to begin with." He licked off the spoon and put it into the sink. "I don't know if I can allow her to snoop around unsupervised."

"Okay." Zoe remained annoyingly calm, as if defusing something explosive. "Then why *did* you offer to employ her?"

Theo threw his hands up. "You said it yourself. We need her to save the gardens—"

"Right," Zoe cut in. "I want you to listen for a second. We've been friends forever, so I'm going to overstep here and give you some advice." She allowed the spoons she was using to rest in the bowl and looked him straight in the eyes. "Focus on the plantation. It's the real treasure here, not some old wives' tale of hidden treasure." She wiped her hands on her apron. "And if you control your temper, you may find that you save more than just the trees."

He blew out a breath. "You're probably right." He laid a hand on Zoe's shoulder. "Thanks for keeping me grounded." He'd needed the venting situation more than anything. "I'm going to go find her. See you later."

Back outside, the afternoon humidity tugged on his skin with familiarity. Seeing Emma, he strode over to where she was plucking some weeds from the limp peonies at the side of the parking lot. She stood when he reached her.

An escaped lock of hair brushed across her porcelain cheek in the soft breeze, and Theo could almost picture her in an antebellum ball gown, her hair pulled up off her shoulders. He shook his head. Romantic notions like this weren't going to help with the garden or the mystery.

When Emma had shown him her great-grandfather's

journal, Theo had had the feeling there was something she was holding back. There had to be more about the situation than metal lock covers and matching hinges—though seeing the sketch had raised the hairs on the back of his neck. Not only did he want to hire her for the grounds, but the lure of mystery and adventure were too much to pass up.

Theo stepped close enough to her that he noticed a slight scent of flowers and wondered if it was the plants or the girl. "Walk with me?" He tipped his head to the right, pointing out where he wanted to walk.

Her hazel eyes searched his face through her glasses, and his heartbeat sped up. At least she didn't seem to know she had power over him. Her lips lifted slightly, and she fell into step beside him.

"Not only do we have overgrowth . . ." he said, hoping he sounded casual and confident. It wasn't often anyone pulled him from his game. "Zoe mentioned you might know what's wrong with our trees?"

He set off for the double row of live oaks. The grandest part of the entire plantation. While the trees weren't unique to Indigo Pointe, it was there that he felt claustrophobic in his contemporaneousness, overwhelmed with the history of the place.

He heard Emma draw in a breath as they stepped past the fence, steeped in lichen and grayed with age. Together, they ducked under the canopy of the live oaks.

Spanish moss dripped from the branches, swirling like kite tails in the breeze. As they walked along the dirt road, he wondered at the number of people who might have also walked this very lane—not only the countless tourists over the years, but those who had worked, lived, played, and visited—all the while with these same eighty-two trees stretched above, offering shelter from the weather, a hiding place, a clandestine meeting place, a refuge from the world.

"Yes," Emma said, so softly he almost missed it. "I can save your trees."

He felt her relief, and his own, mingling with those ghosts of the past. They walked several more yards, almost reaching the end of the lane. One turn, and they'd be back at the parking lot, back into what always felt like stepping from history into the present. He wasn't sure he was ready to make that transition yet without making sure he wasn't going to lose Emma.

"Does that mean you're considering the job?"

"No matter what I decide about the job, Theo, I won't allow these trees to die."

He knew she wouldn't. But that wasn't the same as agreeing to take the job. He needed to up his game.

"There's something I need you to consider before making your decision." He made it sound serious, like this might deter her from taking the job, but if he read her right, this would be the carrot to entice her. "Did you notice the gate in front?"

He put a hand on Emma's elbow to turn her gently toward the front of the property, hoping the touch wouldn't scare her off. They couldn't really see the gate from here, especially with those awful evergreen bushes masking it, but they had a great view of the patchy grass. Such an open expanse was completely out of place.

"Yes . . ."

The woman was cautious, but at the same time, curious. He was playing this just right. "And the boring lawn between it and the big house?" He waited for her response, keeping his hand at her elbow.

"Umm-hmm."

"That blank slate would be yours to fill." He watched her try to bite back a smile, and continued spelling out his offer. "Without a grand entrance, we're missing out on an important opportunity. It needs something, but not just anything. It has to be just right." He paused, letting her think about it for a few seconds. "After what I saw in your sketchbook this morning, I think you're the perfect person to design it."

CHAPTER 7

Boy, he knew how to get her. Emma admitted to herself that he had looks in abundance and charm when he wanted to, but she could see through that. No, it wasn't that. Theo had her because he'd taken note of her interests and needs, her love of history and plants. Having complete creative control over a historical garden like this one had been a dream of hers for a while now. Not only that, but it would be a gem of a résumé builder.

The timing, too, couldn't have been more perfect. She'd been able to take this vacation because she was between grad school and finding the perfect job, and now, here it was, being dropped into her lap. With strings attached, maybe, but still. She had to stay here, and she knew Theo knew it. She just hoped he wouldn't take advantage of that, but how could he? He was offering a job. A dang good one. Was there a downside?

Butterflies of excitement fluttered through Emma, followed quickly by a slide show of ideas for the grand front entrance. While she hadn't come to Louisiana for a job, she seriously considered accepting.

She and Theo wended their way around the property so Emma could get a better picture of what the job entailed. Overall, it wasn't as bad as it could have been. Neglect was the biggest culprit, though adding a touch of color to offset all the green would help. And definitely some indigo. Indigo Pointe Plantation must include actual indigo.

Emma followed Theo into the ticket office, watching the dust motes swirl in the current when he forced the door open.

"If you'll hand me your keys, I don't mind going back for your car," Theo offered.

Fishing her keys from the bottom of her cloth messenger bag took a second, but Emma located them and handed them to Theo, tingles going up her arm as her fingers brushed across the warmth of his palm.

As soon as he ducked back out of the office, Zoe peeked through another doorway, a plate of cranberry hootycreeks in hand. "Is it safe to come out?"

Emma laughed. "If you're asking if the coast is clear, Theo's gone."

Zoe and her plate of sweet-smelling goodies floated toward her. "Cookie?"

"Thank you." Emma picked one up, pleased to find it was still warm. One bite and she was in heaven.

"You're afraid of him even when you have cookies?"

She wanted it to sound like a joke, but in her mind, she wondered if there was a reason to be afraid. Who was the real Theo? Was it the intimidating Theo with the edgy temper, or the man who kindly showed her the grounds and sought her help to revive the dying plantation?

The idea of being the designer to create Indigo Pointe's grand entrance had Emma giddy, almost to the point of fainting. What kept her from jumping up and down in acceptance was remembering how they'd gotten to this point. Theo had tried to soften the job proposal with levelheaded discussion, but she hadn't forgotten that at first it had been less of an offer and more of an ultimatum.

And then, how could she work for someone that everyone seemed to hate?

"Afraid?" Zoe chuckled. "Of Theo?" Her expressive green eyes were offset beautifully by her caramel skin and plum lipstick. "No one who really knows Theo is afraid of him. No, I wanted to make sure you and I had a chance to grab a cookie or two before he scarfed them all." She lifted a cookie and took a small bite. "To be fair, these are his favorites."

Emma narrowed her eyes, watching Zoe for signs of lying, but the woman didn't seem to notice. She seemed comfortable, happy.

"Seems you might have gotten the wrong impression?" Zoe turned to fill two glasses from a dispenser of iced lemon water on the buffet.

Emma accepted the glass gratefully. "How was I supposed to take it when I heard him fire his tour guide, then get all ticked at me for taking a simple picture of a doorknob or corner me into working for him—not to mention the rumors around town . . ."

"Whoa!" Zoe held up a hand to slow Emma down. "Admittedly, I wasn't there for about half of that, but trust me." Zoe tugged at the amulet on a leather cord around her neck. "He's not that bad once you get to know him."

"Not *that* bad," Emma muttered, loud enough for Zoe to hear. "Just sort of bad."

Zoe chuckled again, the sound soothing. "Oh, girl, you know that's not what I said . . . or what I meant."

Emma liked this woman. "How long have you known him?" Emma set her glass on the counter.

"Since about second grade." Zoe had that look in her eye like she was remembering. "I was the dodgeball queen back when they let kids play dodgeball at school. And he was never afraid to take me on. Even though I beat him every single time." Her pride in this achievement was strong despite the fact that it had to have been forever ago. "And then he up and moved to some dumb boarding school for rich preps in England or somewhere." Zoe rolled her eyes. "We reconnected through a mutual friend in high school when he came home for holidays, and have been best friends ever since."

Thinking back to the "Mr. Lambert" stuff, that was the last thing Emma had expected. "So no truth to the whole beast thing?" She tried to laugh it off.

Zoe pursed her lips and shook her head. "He's misunderstood. That's what he is. But don't tell him I said that. He'd kill me if he thought I made him sound like some sappy emo or something." She took another bite of her cookie. "You might want to grab another cookie." She handed Emma a napkin. "Wrap it up and save it for later. Here he comes."

Emma did as instructed but also listened for any indication that Theo was nearby. Not one pop of gravel, no purr of an engine.

The door screeched against the warped wood floor, making Emma jump. "So, Miss Treager, do we have a deal?" Theo handed her the keys and then headed straight to the cookies.

Before he could grab one, Zoe snatched the plate out of reach. "Is that any way to ask?"

He gave Zoe a side-armed hug while reaching for the plate, successful because his arm was longer than hers. "Hello, my favorite, awesomest cook. May I please have one of these offerings of deliciousness?"

Without waiting for an answer, Theo grabbed two cookies, stacking them one on top of the other and taking a big bite. He turned back to Emma, raising his eyebrows in question as he chewed and swallowed.

"I'll need a place to stay for an extended period of time."

He grinned, a big kid who'd gotten his way. "You can have the east garçonnière. It's fully furnished, and you should be quite comfortable."

She had no objection.

"Then you can start immediately." He took another bite of his cookies.

The guy was nuts. Did he not see how she was dressed? "I need to check out of my hotel and change."

He nodded. "Of course. Be back for dinner." He grabbed Zoe's glass of water and took a gulp.

How dare he? "Doesn't the place have its own kitchen?" It was never going to work if there wasn't.

"Ehh." He made a not-so-much, *kinda-sorta* motion with his head. "A small fridge and a toaster oven, but

Zoe cooks for me and whoever else is on site that day. You'll just eat with us."

She noticed it wasn't exactly a request.

She took her own bite of cookie to buy her a little more time.

Picturing the before and after photos she'd have of the front entrance convinced her, and she could use the money. She had everything she needed and then some.

"You've got yourself a deal, Mr. Lambert."

CHAPTER 8

"Here I am, reporting for duty." Emma plunked her suitcase on the wooden floor beside the ticket counter the next day, smiling at her new boss. Confidence was key, she reminded herself, trying to pretend she wasn't worried about having upset him already.

Okay, so she was, well, probably a full eighteen hours later than what Theo had expected when they'd come to an agreement the previous night. She probably should have gotten his phone number or something, but she hadn't exactly liked that he had been so demanding. He'd ordered her to be back in time for dinner, but for goodness' sake, it was already dinnertime when she left. So she stayed near New Orleans, had a good breakfast, packed up, and arrived at Indigo Pointe after lunch.

"Where have you been?" He wasn't explosive when he asked, but she could tell he was annoyed.

"I had to take care of my hotel and rental car and arrange for a ride out here . . . and it was already late when I left last night—"

"Text me next time." Theo cut off her words and her excuse. "What's your number?" With his stiff, no-nonsense business manner, he punched in the numbers, and she received a text from his phone. Theo picked up her suitcase and pushed the door open with exasperation. "Let's go see your new home."

Emma shrugged off his sullenness, relaxing into the quiet of the plantation. She'd known Theo would react that way and she'd been mentally prepared. She had, after all, defied his orders on principle.

Not knowing what to expect inside a two-hundred-year-old bachelor pad, Emma stood on the porch as Theo unlocked the strangely modern deadbolt and handed her the key. "The room is stocked, but no one's stayed there in a while, so if the AC doesn't work or something, let us know."

She turned back to the closed door in front of her, excited beyond reason to have this little cottage to herself; she just hoped she didn't get freaked out at night being alone in a strange place.

The door swung into an open-concept room, vastly different than she'd imagined. To her right sat a comfortable-looking couch in a soft check of blue and white squares, dotted with red and yellow throw pillows. A squishy overstuffed chair sat in front of a window, open a couple of inches to allow fresh air to blow the gauzy white curtains. That would be the perfect reading nook if she ever had time for books while she was here.

To the left of the front door was a small round wood table flanked with four chairs and topped with a vase of fresh-cut white roses. Zoe must have added the welcoming touch. On the far wall, the small kitchenette was outfitted with only the barest of necessities, just as Theo had explained. She wouldn't starve if she never went up to the office to eat with Zoe and Theo, but she wouldn't eat well. Only so much could be done with a toaster oven and a microwave.

In the back of the cottage was a nice-sized bedroom, a queen-sized four-poster with a fluffy white duvet, a wooden nightstand with another vase of fresh flowers, and an antique wardrobe. The fragrance of the roses followed her as she stuck her head in to check out the bathroom. It was small but contained a tub perfect for soaking, so she'd be good.

Better than good, actually. The garçonnière was a much nicer vacation home than the cheap motel she'd booked for the past week. Fixtures and features had been chosen with comfort in mind, and nothing was overlooked.

After taking a few minutes to unpack and get her things situated, Emma grabbed her sketchpad. This time when she walked the grounds, she would survey the area with a more critical eye, jotting down notes as they occurred to her.

Being out on the grounds, wrapped in a symphony of insects chirping and leaves rustling in the breeze, Emma felt at home. Really, she'd only punished herself by being late. The heat of the day rose as steam from the damp ground, the humidity buzzing with life. She took her time, moving from one section of the property to the next, sketching in flowerbeds and starting a couple of lists to keep her organized. One list was of the products she would need, including fertilizers, herbicides, and organic insecticides. The other list contained things that needed done that she would later prioritize according to urgency and seasonal timetables. So far, the rose garden and live oaks needed her attention first.

She'd rounded almost the entire property—leaving out the actual plantation fields, which of course wouldn't be her job—when she arrived at the large barn to see what kinds of tools were at her disposal. Wrapping a hand around the huge iron handle, Emma yanked, setting the sliding door into motion. Light flooded in and she stepped back in awe. Of course a plantation this size would need combines and tractors, but with the antebellum feel of the place, she'd somehow forgotten real time and found herself unprepared for the modern sight.

A row of pegs held shovels, rakes, and hoes trapped in upright positions. Above the pegs, a shelf held bottles of plant care solutions, hand trowels, and pruners—just out of reach for someone her height. She tipped up on her toes, stretching with all her might and a puff of indignation. Snagging the closest shears, she rocked back on her heels before testing the tool's action and sharpness. These would do. She struggled to replace them on the shelf, then struck them off her list with a line.

"Finding what you need?"

The man needed to quit sneaking up on her. It was as if he didn't trust her.

"Yes. Thank you." Emma made another note, this one more nonsense than anything, but it kept her from looking at Theo. She didn't want to risk revealing the fact that he made her heart pound in nervousness. Or was it something else?

"I thought you'd be working already." He pointed to her sketchpad as if she were taking a leisure day to draw for pleasure.

"I am working." Growing up with brothers, she

knew how to claim authority by throwing a mean glare. "Creation takes seven stages." She crossed her index fingers, ready to count them out. "First, the idea. Second, the plan."

She shook her notebook and then tucked it under her arm again to point at the third finger. "Third, you gather the materials. Fourth, you 'do the work.' Fifth, evaluate—observe what works and what doesn't. Sixth, revise the plan according to your evaluation, and seventh, enjoy the fruits of your labor."

Emma stopped and tapped her finger against the notebook. "Technically, there are more like fourteen stages because I do everything on paper first, making sure everything will work before you do it physically." Theo had probably stopped listening to her four steps ago, and she needed to grab his attention again.

"Right now I'm assessing the materials." She ruffled a few of the pages she'd written on already, exposing her lists.

Theo nodded slowly. "If you say so . . ."

She gave him a questioning look, waiting for him to argue with her process. Surely he couldn't come up with an exception.

"How do you enjoy something on paper before you've actually done the work?" A mischievous glint came to his eye, and he scrubbed a hand through his short, sandy hair.

So he had been listening. The realization made her happier than it should have. "It makes sense if you think about it." Hearing herself, she blanched. She'd been so distracted by his looks, she had insulted him. She quickly hurried to explain. "You're trying to tell me you've never planned something out, imagining how someone would react? A special date, perhaps?" She felt the familiar blush coming on and turned away, trying to find something so she would appear busy. "You go through each step, thinking about what might or might not be the results. I have to ask things like, will it be comfortable? Is it functional? Will it be beautiful year-round?" She could go on, but he was finally nodding in understanding.

"Ah, I see. So you daydream."

"I wouldn't call it that." Was it that hard to admit she was a professional who knew what she was doing? But he was teasing, and she knew that. "Other than the leaf blister on the live oaks, are there any other problem areas?"

"You noticed the roses too." Theo squeezed his eyes shut as if picturing the property in his mind. "Actually, yes. I noticed a problem with the flowerbeds by the gazebo. Will you come take a look?"

The walk over was a bit of a trek. "More wilting? Or premature browning?" While they walked, Emma thought she might as well get a head start trying to figure out what the problem might be.

"No. More like missing petals," Theo explained.

They cut through the center of the parterre garden that Emma would never tire of seeing and then through the grass, badly in need of a trim. "Maybe something's eating them?"

A couple of live oaks—younger than those that formed the grand allée, but easily a century old themselves—created a soft canopy above the gazebo, dappling the ground with sunshine. At least they looked unaffected by the leaf wilt the other trees were suffering.

A clump of Spanish moss fell from the tree above them.

"Zoe?" Theo asked, incredulous as he looked up. "What are you doing up there?"

Apparently this wasn't an everyday occurrence.

Zoe sat on the branch closest to the ground, though it was high enough it was a wonder Zoe had been able to get up there without a ladder. She hid her hands behind her back, but that only made Emma more curious to catch a glimpse of what she was holding.

Theo stepped around so he could see behind her. "Is that a sandwich?"

"Fine." Defeated, Zoe moved her hands, and her sandwich, into her lap.

"Hungry?" Theo teased. "Because I don't think trees eat sandwiches."

"Ha ha." Zoe didn't allow a real laugh, but her sarcasm was light and teasing. "If you must know, I was feeding the squirrels."

"A sandwich?" How Theo could ask this with a straight face was beyond Emma. She was already sucking in her cheeks to keep from laughing.

Zoe shrugged. "They like peanut butter sandwiches." She sighed. "A few of the squirrels will come up to me at the office, but sometimes I like to meet them where they are." Zoe pulled off about an inch-sized piece to show Theo and Emma. "When I'm up in the tree, they're more likely to take it from my hands." She reached up, cooing in a soft voice, "Come on, Chip, come here."

Theo's smile grew wider with every passing moment. "You know if you feed them, you're asking for trouble."

"Trouble?" Zoe shook her head, her long waves bouncing around her shoulders. "They're sweet, not trouble."

"Maybe making sandwiches is no trouble, but having them here . . . they'll take over the place." Theo looked almost afraid to ask Emma. "You're the gardener. What do you think?"

He probably thought because she was female, she

had a weakness for all things furry and fuzzy, but squirrels were awful pests for gardens. They broke hedges, chewed on new growth, and stole flower bulbs. She'd spent her short-lived career so far experimenting with garlic and cayenne pepper and other natural remedies to repel the vermin, but if they messed with her too much out here, she'd be dangerously close to purchasing an air gun to ward them off. But that didn't change the fact that she thought this situation with Zoe was the cutest thing she'd ever seen. Kind of like Cinderella feeding the mice. Someday those squirrels just might save her.

"Squirrels wreak havoc on gardens. Worst arborists ever, truth be told. They are hard workers and successful—too successful—but they never consult my plans." She shrugged a shoulder. "But you can't control everything." Getting rid of squirrels wouldn't keep trees from sprouting in undesirable areas, plus she didn't want to offend Zoe. "No harm done, I'm sure."

"Speaking of lunch, did you get any?" Zoe asked, climbing down from the tree.

Before Emma could respond, her stomach growled so loudly, Theo had to overhear.

He turned to Zoe. "Lunch is over. I guess she won't be late next time." His tone was joking, but a tension was evident, a reminder that she'd ignored his instructions.

Fine, whatever. Emma pulled a sweet and salty

peanut bar from her satchel and ripped it open. Although she wasn't that hungry yet, taking a bite while pointedly glaring at Theo made the bar taste that much better. It wasn't like she was going to starve. She could take care of herself.

While chewing the bite, she snugged the wrapper back over the exposed end and tucked it back into her bag for later. She opened her sketchbook to the next page and retrieved the pencil that had been securing her hair up off her neck, allowing her long locks to tumble down her back. "Thank you for the conversation, but I need to get back to work."

She was pretty sure Theo could feel the brush-off. At least, she hoped he did.

"The affected plants are over there." Theo pointed to the hydrangea bushes that skirted the gazebo. While they added some color, they weren't quite right for the setting and were obviously a favorite of the squirrels. She could find a better solution.

"Thanks for bringing it to my attention." If he wanted to be cold, she could shoot it right back at him.

CHAPTER 9

Theo had known as soon as he'd made the comment about Emma missing lunch yesterday that he'd blown it. Big time. He was just trying to make a joke, after all, playing on the fact that everyone talked as if he were a beast. But then Emma had taken him seriously and gotten all offended. If she couldn't take a little joke, he had better things to do.

But it still bugged him. Obviously. Here it was the next morning, and he was still stewing over it.

He ran the beard trimmer over his face quickly, enough to tame the excess growth of the past couple of days. He'd take the time to shave this weekend for sure. Putting everything away, he grabbed a ball cap and jammed it on his head as he left his loft and jogged down the staircase open to the rest of his New Orleans home.

The house, a traditional Creole two-story smack-dab in the middle of the noisy French Quarter, had been left to him when his dad tired of the States and moved to Europe for good. It made sense. More and more of his father's business meetings were there, and it was a lot more fun to meet over good food than conferencing over video.

Theo, too, liked the traveling part of their joint international real estate business. He also loved owning houses in several countries. Visiting each gave him the mixed sense of adventure and feeling of home each time he transitioned from one to the next.

This New Orleans home, though, was Theo's new favorite. Not one for crowds or Mardi Gras—Theo planned to avoid it during that busy time—but he loved New Orleans for plenty of other reasons. The city was full of history, intrigue, and unique culture, but it also was as close to a home as he'd had in his life. It was the home he returned to every break from school growing up.

Recently, though, when his father had passed it down to him, Theo had had the house completely gutted and remodeled, and he couldn't be more pleased with how it turned out. Up-and-coming architect Keenan Perry had designed the overhaul. Almost every part of the interior was removed, including most of the second floor, before being rebuilt into an opulent, modern space.

Large mullioned windows topped with arches allowed light to flood into the room. A master suite filled a loft on one side of the house, facing a two-story wall of books on the other, with an elegant wrought iron staircase that circled up to a narrow walkway for access.

Originally the home had belonged to his grandparents and eventually, it became Theo's father's inheritance as the younger brother. Theo's uncle, the elder of the brothers, had received the plantation home next to Indigo Pointe, though the main house was little more than a small farmhouse in comparison.

Through the twentieth century, as his family purchased plots from Indigo Pointe's fields, they were able to merge the plantations into one very profitable business. At the same time, the Lamberts carefully cultivated marriages, meticulous educations, and advantageous business ventures. In the last few years, they continued to build their empire around the world, but the final piece of Indigo Pointe, the plantation house itself, had always been frustratingly, elusively, out of reach.

Truth be told, the fact that the main buildings had been the one holdout from the Lamberts having the whole plantation was a big reason Theo had wanted the property, but being there, feeling its history, hearing his family stories, knowing there was something different about the place, was what had sparked his interest in preserving history and, later, his career in real estate law and investment. It had been a lucrative profession, and he never lost his interest in saving Indigo Pointe.

It seemed to have taken the Treagers a while to catch on to what the Lamberts were doing, but once they realized and knew the Lamberts wanted to buy the big house on Indigo Pointe, the Treagers sold out to someone else solely out of spite. It was an awful shame that almost ruined the property completely because, as far as Theo knew, the new owner never came by the place more than once every few years.

It didn't matter. Theo had won in the end, though it took years of effort and an exorbitant price—but then money was never the object standing in his way these days. Falling in love with the wrong girl, though, that could be a problem—as could messing it up with the right girl before he even got the chance.

Theo had messed up way too many times to count with Emma the last few days. Well, with everyone, really. And just like the once dilapidated New Orleans home, he needed to fix things, make them better than they ever were. Perhaps a complete overhaul.

He didn't want to push Emma away. There was

something he really liked about her. She was beautiful, witty, smart, creative, and well, just plain nice. For one thing, there was no way a horticulturist would like squirrels, and he saw in her eyes exactly how she felt about those darn rodents, but she took Zoe's side anyway. And not once had she called Theo out on his anger, though she made her feelings known. Each of these situations added another layer to the person he wanted to get to know. What could he do to repair the damage he'd already done?

He had a sudden flash of inspiration. Beignets. No one could resist beignets, and it was possible he could be the one to introduce her to their deliciousness. That would make an apology go a little easier, wouldn't it?

CHAPTER 10

Theo wrestled with the office door that morning as usual, noisily announcing his arrival, which was why he was surprised to overhear a snippet of conversation Emma probably had wanted to keep from him. She hadn't asked him this particular question.

"Do you know of any locked gates or doors on the property?" Emma was asking Zoe. "Maybe a hidden tunnel or even a small cabinet?"

The woman was all over the map with possibilities, but it all came back to looking for more of the lock covers. Zoe wouldn't know. She spent most of her time at the ticket office and museum looking at spreadsheets and accounts, cleaning up the books and crafting business plans to work out all of Indigo Pointe's kinks. He couldn't fault Emma for trying, though.

He allowed the echo of his feet on the wooden plank floor to telegraph his arrival, taking care to step with extra force. As he'd expected, Emma's questions remained unanswered, the topic abandoned.

"Thanks for the orange juice," Theo heard Emma say on the other side of the door. "I've never taken the time to squeeze my own."

Theo heard the scraping of a chair and hurried through the doorway. "Before you go . . ." He took a quick breath, afraid to lose her. "I brought beignets." He stepped over to the table where the women had been sitting and set the bag on the table top.

"Chocolate or regular?" Zoe eyed him with suspicion. She hated the chocolate ones, but they were his favorite.

"Ah, come on, Zo, give me some credit. I can be a nice guy sometimes." He offered her his best cheesy grin. "I brought both."

"Word to the wise," Zoe told Emma conspiratorially, "eventually you'll want to try both, but you can't beat the original."

Emma peeked into the bag, the dark and light donut squares nestled together under a blanket of sprinkled powdered sugar. A diabetic coma in a bag. She pulled a light square from the bag and took a bite, eliciting the biggest real smile he'd seen from her since she'd discovered the lock cover.

"Amazing," she said around another bite. He hoped they were still warm enough so they would be their best.

Emma had on a pair of faded jeans, a small rip in one knee, a streak of mud already on them. "Have you been out working already?"

"Are you kidding?" Zoe said. "She had a pile of weeds and cut branches five feet high by the time I pulled in this morning."

He was impressed. He was nowhere near a morning person himself.

"Early morning is the best time. The ground is soft, the weeds easier to pull, the snail problem easier to assess, and the temperature much more livable."

"Snail problem?" Even if he'd seen a snail, it never would have occurred to him that it would be a problem.

"Just a small one?" She was so sweet, trying to make sure he wouldn't be offended by her observation.

"A small snail?" He couldn't help but goad her.

"A slight small snail problem," she teased back, catching on quickly. Her dimples showed when she tried not to smile. It was the most adorable thing he'd seen in a long time. And something he vowed to see more of.

"You mean a scant slight small snail squeeze?" He

couldn't believe he'd been able to say that mouthful without laughing.

"I hope I don't have to resort to squeezing them." She made an exaggerated face as if encountering something particularly revolting. "I happen to have a scant slight small snail solution to our . . . scrape?"

She'd been confident until she had to concentrate so hard on finding another *s* word for problem. Knowing he couldn't top that one, Theo shook his head in concession and they all burst into laughter.

"There's a lot of work that needs done. *A lot.*" She took another bite of her beignet, chewed slowly, and swallowed, clearly hesitant to say what was on her mind. "How long has it been since you've had a landscaper? There's more work than one person can do, I'm afraid." Her face flushed scarlet, and she started talking again, her words coming quick and animated. "Not that I can't do it. I can. It will take me a while, though, you know, if you can't afford another person."

Relief flooded through him. Being able to afford someone wasn't the problem. With the state she found the property in, he could see why she would think that, but he waved off her concern.

"Of course. I expected to." He felt the need to rationalize the state of the property—explain why the place was a shambles. "I just bought the place. The last owner lived two thousand miles away, and the only thing he ever did with the estate was shoot an antebellum zombie movie that never made it off the B rolls. Our deal closed a couple of weeks ago. My aim now is to restore it without losing the integrity or history of the place, and if that means getting you some help, that's not a problem."

He wouldn't hire just anyone, though.

"So what is your vision for the garden?" she asked. "Sort of like a miniature Longwood Gardens?" She had a twinkle in her eye, a challenge. She probably thought he had no idea where that one was.

"If only this garden could compare." Over the years, he'd visited plenty of gardens, and it took a second to detangle the details of the Pennsylvania garden she'd referenced from the rest. "But if we're going for the best parterre gardens, I was thinking more like Levens Hall or Eyrignac Manor. If we want to rebrand past live oaks and hedges, we could shoot for something like Wales's Bodnant Gardens or Keukenhof."

The opportunity to take in the sights was what Theo loved most about traveling. In his mind's eye, he recalled traversing the meticulously planned paths of each of these gardens, admiring the fragrances, textures, and sights. But it wasn't until he'd experienced the neglected potential of Indigo Pointe that he fully appreciated the investment of work that transformed land into works of art.

When he finished speaking, Emma was wiping her sticky fingers on a paper napkin, her eyes wide with awe.

See, they did have things in common, he wanted to point out, but he didn't.

"I'm not sure we could pull off the tulip gardens in this climate, but we're not too far off the tree tunnels at Bodnant."

He loved their linguistic dances about snails and gardens, and he couldn't wait to see what the next obscure conversation would be about. He was pretty sure she had just captured his heart.

CHAPTER 11

How much money did this guy have? Had he visited all those places or merely done his research online? Emma was about to ask when Theo changed the subject.

"I need this property to reach its full potential as soon as possible."

How had he gone from talking excitedly about famous European gardens to beating the dead horse of his "get it done now, get it done right" mantra? Emma forced herself not to roll her eyes.

"Why?" She hoped she didn't sound like she was challenging him. "Do you plan to sell?"

"It's what I do." He was matter-of-fact about the situation, and the thought scared her to death.

What would happen if it sold? Would she ever solve

her grandfather's puzzle? Not that she had one iota of say in the matter. "What about the family connection?"

For the first time since she'd known him, Theo looked startled by the question, almost taken aback. "What family connection?" he asked slowly.

She had listened during his presentation. Had she misunderstood?

"It's not a family plantation," he said. "I just told you I recently purchased it."

"Yes, but . . ." Emma tried to recall any of the names she'd seen on the linage plaque posted inside the big house. He'd distracted her so thoroughly by standing right behind her, the scent of his cologne and the heat of his body more captivating than names she couldn't focus on. And she'd been distraught by their run-in over the photograph. "You mentioned forced heirships and that it has been a working plantation since the late 1700s, so I guess I figured you purchased it from a relative."

She closed her eyes, remembering the framed lineage, feeling the movement of the words as if they were calligraphy. Something was on the tip of her memory; she could almost grasp it. "Wait. Did I see Treager on that list?" How had that crucial detail slipped her notice? "Did Indigo Pointe belong to *my* family at one point?"

"About that . . ."

The man was struggling, but she wasn't going to let him off the hook. She glared at him. "Why didn't you tell me?"

"You were looking at the pedigree. I assumed you saw your own name there on the list. That kind of thing tends to stand out to people." Though he seemed nervous about it, his words made sense.

She felt a surge of envy for something she hadn't even thought to want a half hour before. Yes, she liked the place. Yes, she wanted the history preserved. Yes, she felt a familial connection, but she hadn't realized how deeply her roots here went. A sense of loss washed over her, but she tried to suppress it.

Perhaps Indigo Pointe had belonged to her ancestors, but not once could she ever remember the name even being whispered at a family reunion. Until recently, no one had mentioned being from Louisiana. No one spoke of sugarcane instead of sugar beets or indigo instead of mint. How could she feel she had lost something that had never belonged to her?

How could she hold that against Theo, who had purchased the property to preserve it, preventing it from slipping into the chasm of irrevocable disrepair? That wouldn't be fair of her.

She took another sip of orange juice to give herself an extra moment to think. Avoidance. That was almost always the best course of action. "If we could hire some guys to come out and help me clean up the live oaks, the trees will quickly be on the mend. The next highest task on my priority list is the roses. They need . . . well, everything . . . before it gets too much later into the summer."

Theo raised his eyebrows as he listened, closed-mouthed. She couldn't blame him. She changed moods and subjects as quickly as he did.

"I'll be in the rose garden if you need me." Emma stepped to the sink and rinsed her glass before drying her hands on her jeans. "Thanks for breakfast."

She exited through the back door and closed it quietly behind her.

CHAPTER 12

That first step onto the porch of the garçonnière every morning would never get old. Glistening fog shrouded the gardens, cloaked the marble statue, and obscured the sundial. Emma didn't need the sun to tell her it was early. Indigo Pointe was magical before visitors showed up, the silence disturbed by only the whispers of forgotten memory. The rest of the world was only a few minutes away by car but eons away in her mind.

Emma could get used to living at Indigo Pointe for the long haul if only the work weren't so strenuous. Sore muscles tugged her skin taut as if she no longer fit into her own body; however, the evidence of yesterday's bending and lifting also filled her with a deep feeling of accomplishment.

She locked her front door and pocketed the key, stretching and leaning back in an arch. The three paces it took for her to approach the stairs were just enough to reveal a resin garden gnome waiting by the porch railing. Armed with a miniature hoe and watering can, the chubby-cheeked statue was an unconventional modern-day statue in this Greek Revival courtyard. The irony of the juxtaposition wasn't lost on her. Was it Theo or Zoe who had put it here?

Smiling to herself at his presence, Emma left the gnome at his station and headed to the barn to retrieve her tools. The lawn crew wasn't scheduled to come until tomorrow, when she would oversee their trimming of the precious live oaks. Until then, she would continue in the rose garden, where she'd worked so hard the previous day. By her calculations, she'd have at least two more days before they would be ready for her to spread her attentions elsewhere in the garden.

Reaching the white barn with its deep green trim, Emma tugged on the door and found another gnome frozen as he went about his yard work. The pudgy fellow rode a tricycle that transported a bucket of yellow resin flowers on the back and small hand tools in the faux wicker basket on the handlebars.

"Already working hard, are you?" she greeted the statue as if he could hear and respond. She picked him up from the doorway, staring into his unblinking, almost disturbing eyes, but with the jolly smile, how could he be anything but cute? "Come on, little guy, we need to move you out of harm's way."

After positioning him near a fence post, Emma collected her tools and made her way to the rose garden, on the lookout for more gnomes. These kinds of things always went in threes, didn't they? It wasn't until she stepped through the arbor archway into the churchyard that she was rewarded. In the churchyard alone, she found a set of three gnomes, each riding a different animal—a dove, a snail, and a turtle. She left them where they were, occasionally talking to them as she worked. It was crazy, but it helped pass the time, and she found she rather liked them.

She'd made significant progress in her work as the sun had stretched across the horizon by the time Theo ducked under the arbor and into the solitude of the rose garden.

"Ready for a break?" Theo handed her a water bottle slick with condensation, and she realized how much she needed it.

"Thanks." She accepted the bottle and drank deeply. "What time is it?"

"Time for lunch." His body language, though, said the opposite. He settled himself on the soft Kentucky bluegrass that had been beckoning her for a nap.

"Looking good! I can't believe the transformation already."

"Thanks." Emma flopped down next to him, all of a sudden exhausted. "There's still so much more to do."

She had been working since six. She eyed the bushes critically, but had to agree with Theo's assessment. She'd started on one end, painstakingly clipping away sucker branches and overgrowth as she moved down the line. It looked like a homeless man was getting a much-needed haircut and shave, but only one side of his head and face had been done so far.

"I see what you're saying about that snail problem." Theo pointed with his chin at the gnome astride the giant snail. "But it's a little bigger than you let on." He took a drink from his own water bottle.

She nodded in mock solemnity. "That's what happens when you allow it to get out of control."

"Looks like the gnome's got him in hand. The bridle kind of gives that impression."

"True." She lay back on the grass, the warmth of the sun putting her at risk for falling asleep.

A couple of blissfully silent seconds ticked by before she felt Theo rise. "Ready?" he whispered, barely interrupting the stillness.

Emma wasn't sure she could lift herself off the ground, but he offered her a hand and a power boost. The soft coolness of his palm against her callused one made her almost unwilling to let go. She'd barely turned around when she noticed the first gnome from her porch tucked behind the base of the arbor vine.

"How'd he get here?" Not that she expected an answer.

"Gnomes aren't to be seen by the tourists," he explained simply. "They lose their magic if they're caught by the guests."

Emma nodded. "That makes sense, but how did he end up here?"

"You said you needed help?" Theo asked as if it were a question. Silly man. He was grasping at straws, but he was so cute.

Emma gathered her tools, tucking them out of the way for later, and they started toward the office. "Do you plan on restoring the overseer's house or any of the other dependencies?"

"Sort of." Theo kicked one of the larger rocks like a soccer ball. "It is important for the building exteriors to be in good order—not updated, but cared for—but I don't plan on adding any of them to the tour. Because of that, I figure it's okay to go for functional rather than restored. You know, things like indoor plumbing and air conditioning. Once I get back to my day job, Zoe will be running the show, so I promised her first dibs on which one will be her permanent residence. I think she's taking the farmhouse, but she hasn't made a decision yet. I told her she needs to get a move on, but she says she can't find the right general contractor." He shrugged like it was no big deal.

"She's not in a huge hurry, though, since she's always lived in the area." He cut in front of her half a step to get to his rock just as she was about to step there. She grabbed on to his arm to keep from stumbling, and she loved the way he paused to steady her. "Sorry about that," he said, but kept going, seemingly less affected by their touch than she felt. "As far as other buildings, eventually I expect we'll fix them up for visiting family members, the maintenance-slash-handyman, and my uncle who manages the fields."

"I thought you said you were going to sell." She was confused. Had he recently changed his mind?

"Did I say that?" His innocent look was way too forced.

"And I quote, 'It's what I do.'" Emma's deep "man voice" came out too gravelly, and Theo laughed.

"I did say that, didn't I?" He shook his head. "No, that was never actually the plan with this property."

Though she wanted to explore the why behind previously misleading her, she wanted to get back to the earlier conversation more. "So you're not going to do the restoration work yourself?" She didn't think he would, but she liked teasing him about it.

"Ha ha," he said sarcastically. He kicked his rock a

little too hard, and it ended up too far out of his reach. "As you seem to have guessed, I don't really do that kind of thing." He looked at her sideways. "I'm more of a 'paper-pusher businessman with a little tour guiding on the side' kind of guy, but renovation and landscape architecture? That's better left up to the professionals."

"Thank you. I guess?" Emma wasn't sure if he was complimenting her.

"I know my limitations. I want things done impeccably and I am well aware I couldn't deliver. So I hire the best. My contributions consist of signing plans and signing checks to people much more creative than I." He got a faraway look in his eyes as if remembering a specific project. "And then it gets carried out flawlessly. Win-win."

Back at the office, he forced open the sticky front door instead of leading them around the back, and they walked through. "One of my next orders of business is finding the right handyman for this huge job."

A thought occurred to Emma, so perfect she was almost afraid to present it. "About the handyman-slash-GC Zoe is looking for . . . I know a guy who just might be right for the job. My brother Brett is skilled in historic restoration." Having her big brother and best friend here on the family property just felt right. "But . . ."

Would Brett be interested if that meant moving his

family again? He'd done it before. And the Treager plantation. He'd kill her if she didn't at least make the suggestion. "He's currently elbow-deep near Chicago restoring a Frank Lloyd Wright some idiot almost ruined." She closed her eyes, trying to remember. "I think he'll be done by the end of summer, beginning of fall. If you're looking for the right person, a few months isn't too long to wait. I could have him email a résumé and portfolio."

"Do that. We'll work on the grand entrance design while we wait." Theo's eyes darted around and he shifted his weight.

Used to having his full attention, Emma looked around, trying to figure out what was distracting him. She couldn't figure it out. "I do have a preliminary sketch, but I'm not quite ready to present it yet."

"No rush. I don't suppose you've had much time for it yet."

That was true. Coming up with an idea wasn't too hard, but there was a myriad of other things she needed to do to make sure her design was the best it could be. She needed to do internet comparisons, see if anything inspired her in a different direction. Then she needed to choose materials, outline a prospective budget, and timeline. It was a big project, and she wanted to do it right, but it was also going to be so much fun.

Why hadn't they gone into the kitchen? When Theo

had stopped in the office rather than going on into the kitchen, it had felt odd. But maybe he was allowing them privacy to finish their conversation. "Are we . . . waiting for something?" she asked.

He held up a finger, asking her to wait a minute. "Hey, Zoe?" Theo called through to the kitchen. "Can you come out here for a second?"

"About time. Where have y'all been?" Zoe came through the swinging door, her hands full with a plate of club sandwiches and a bowl of fruit salad. "What's up?"

Theo stepped forward to relieve her of the heavy bowl, and the two of them set the food on the sideboard. "Did you see what you've done now?"

Zoe's forehead wrinkled, creating lines between her eyes that made her look twenty years older. "Umm, no? Where? What are you talking about?"

Theo walked the women to the front door, opened it, and pointed behind a thick banana tree trunk near the parking lot. Was that another gnome? Or three?

"What on earth?" Zoe bounded down the stairs, and the other two followed for a closer look.

Two resin squirrels seemed to be walking away from the plantation, a garden gnome hoisted on their shoulders as if they were hauling him off the property. "I told you if you fed them, those squirrels would take over," Theo deadpanned.

Zoe slapped him on his chest. "You joker." She marched back toward the office. "Let's eat before they come back for our food."

"A plethora of gnomes." Emma could pretend seriousness as well as Theo could. "I wonder where they're all coming from." She shook her head at the perfectness of the squirrel statue after Zoe and the peanut butter sandwiches. "You know, I may have to reconsider this job. I didn't realize when I took it on that you have a gnome problem in addition to those pesky snails. I'm afraid I might have missed that section in class about how to deal with gnomes."

Theo grinned. "They can be difficult to get rid of, but maybe you could train them, make them part of your gardening team."

CHAPTER 13

Theo couldn't remember how he'd even come up with the idea of the garden gnomes, but they'd gone over better than planned with Emma and Zoe. He'd found the first set of gnomes at a local garden shop. They were typical and fit what he was looking for, but he'd hit the jackpot when he came across the squirrels carting off the gnome. That had been the absolute best.

He knew Zoe would love them, and Emma—he was starting to figure her out a little more too. He liked this playful side of hers, and now that she was asking where the plethora of gnomes was coming from, he had to get more.

After lunch on his way back to his New Orleans

home for business calls and paperwork, Theo decided a quick detour was in order. He hopped into his pickup and headed straight to Contrary Mary's Nursery.

"Theo! Back again?" The owner was about fifteen years his senior but ever the motherly type. She wiped wet hands on her forest-green apron and adjusted her straw hat so he could see her eyes.

He felt a little guilty that she knew his name, but he hadn't remembered hers. Luckily, she had a name tag on this time. Suzette. "So not Mary, huh?" From the patient look on her face when he said it, she'd probably heard the joke a million times. "Next you're going to tell me you're not even Miss Muffet, I presume."

That earned him a genuine chuckle. "Sadly, no, but I suppose that's good since, being outside and around plants all the time, I see more than my share of spiders. How did the gnomes work out?"

"I had no idea they'd be such a hit." The fact that Suzette was interested made him feel like they were in on it together. He told her about Zoe's reaction to the squirrels. "So now I need more."

Suzette winked at him. "Come. I did some searching in my downtime, in case you swung back by. It was fun," she admitted. She pulled off her straw hat, the band leaving a ring around her close-cropped curls. She waved the hat in front of her, stirring the air. "Can you believe how hot it is already?"

She walked him inside, where sweet air conditioning was blowing. At the cash register, she turned the monitor so they both could see. Clicking one of the tabs opened up more garden gnomes than Theo had ever imagined. The two of them sifted through the images, ordering more than Theo would probably find a use for, but how could he pass up garden ninjas, the gnomes' pointy hats evident under their black hoods, or the grumpy one with a laughable scowl?

This was going to be fun.

"Could you overnight them?" Theo asked, eager to have them at the ready. In the meantime, he needed something for tomorrow morning, and he had an idea.

"Are you sure? Postage won't be cheap." Suzette was also making a commission off of them when he probably could have ordered them himself off the internet, but she had done all of the work of finding them.

"I'm sure, Suzette." He stepped to the nearby display of pots and small statues, perusing her stock until he found what he was looking for. "I'll take these as well."

She added them to the bill, and Theo handed her his platinum credit card.

"We're going to be getting a lot of work done at Indigo Pointe. It might be helpful if I set up a business account with you." Having a good working relationship with his fellow business owners was important to him, especially as he hoped Emma would find herself up here often.

She walked him through the process, and in a few minutes everything was taken care of.

"I'll shoot you a text as soon as your gnomes they come in." Suzette walked Theo out the front door. "See you tomorrow. And I want to hear details."

KNOWING EMMA WOULD BE WORKING in the rose garden again the next day, Theo had surreptitiously banished the old gnomes to the barn in the twilight so he could replace them with his two new ones. While it would have been fun to have Emma discover gnomes elsewhere in the garden, Theo couldn't exactly leave this kind of kitschy stuff in the formal garden where the tourists strolled through a few times a day. Whimsical didn't exactly mesh with the formality of the 1800s. So in all, the rose garden wasn't a bad place to have her working.

"How are the roses this afternoon?" Theo really had no purpose in seeking out Emma while she worked other than that he wanted to spend time with her. "Are the gnomes still being a bother?"

Though Theo had planted the two new statues the previous night, he hadn't planned a way to watch her discover them. He'd started his day early on conference calls from his downtown home an hour away and spent the rest of the morning with his spreadsheets and returning emails and phone calls. He couldn't have his international clients feeling left out as he played around in Louisiana—which was precisely what he'd discovered was happening.

"I'm sorry to say that the gnomes are AWOL today." Emma shook her head, her dark hair bouncing in its ponytail. She wasn't wearing her glasses today, and while he usually liked them, her hazel eyes were even more striking now that he could see them better. "But I did find a clue."

Her exaggerated innocence was entertaining, and her excitement was contagious, especially when she took his hand and led him where he knew they were. It was easy to play along—anything to feel her touch. She stopped in front of a tiny resin house. "I think they live here," she whispered, as if she didn't want to scare them away.

"I think you might be right," he whispered back. She hadn't dropped his hand, and he was careful not to squeeze or remind her in any way that they were still touching. "And what is that?" He used his other hand to point at a tiny bridge he'd placed a few feet away, but something was different.

"Oh, that must be their bridge." Emma tugged on

his hand to drag him closer to it. "There's a canal which sometimes fills with water. The bridge keeps them safe."

"Clearly." The canal was little more than a shallow furrow and hadn't been there the night before. He hadn't even thought about the need for an obstacle to necessitate a bridge.

The gnome topic would soon be used up, and Theo had to find another excuse for staying. "Could you teach me what you're doing here?" He waved his free hand to indicate her work. "I know nothing about caring for roses."

Oh, the lights that sparked in her eyes! He'd asked just the right question. Though she dropped his hand to show him how to use the pruners, it was balanced out as she leaned around him, pointing out where to clip. At first, he was distracted by her closeness, but as they toiled side by side, he realized how satisfying the work was. He looked back at the progress they'd made, pleased that it showed a difference.

As his mother's favorite part of the plantation, saving this rose garden had been of particular concern to Theo when he bought the place. Every day Theo's father had come out to the plantation to help out his brother, he'd gone home with a single champagne-colored rose for his young bride. His mother had started calling them Lambert roses, and Theo had never thought to question this before. He'd ask her next time he brought her out to see the lovely bushes.

"Do you know what would be awesome?" Theo asked, not completely serious. She waited for him to answer. "Alternating purple and yellow roses."

"Really?" The skepticism in her voice was obvious.

"Yeah, LSU colors."

She sighed, exaggerating the sound and shaking her head vehemently. "You shouldn't have said that. The idea was growing on me until I knew why."

"What, not a Tiger fan?"

"While that might be a pretty combination on another part of the property, I like the subtlety of this color scheme." That she completely sidestepped his question did not go unnoticed. "I like how it goes from white to dark." He'd never looked that closely before, but it was nice how there was one plant each of white, cream, champagne, pale pink, peach, orange, salmon, hot pink, and then red in a row. "If we can get the branches to overlap, it'll blend them a little more."

Over the course of the next few hours, Emma taught him how to prune away old woody stems and twiggy growth and then thin out overcrowding. If they trained the lateral shoots to grow horizontally, using garden ties to help them stay after they wound them around the split-rail fence, more blossoms would bud.

"We've fertilized, which will help with color

enhancement, among other things, and we've deadheaded. The last thing we'll do is spray underneath the leaves for blackspot, and we'll be done with the rose garden. Finally."

"You sound like you don't like roses." Theo knew not every woman loved roses best, but he'd grown up with a woman who did. It wouldn't surprise him, however, if Emma didn't. As a horticulturalist, she knew more flower types than pretty much anyone else in the world, so she surely wouldn't go with something so pedestrian . . . or would she consider it classic? What he was quickly learning was that he couldn't even guess what she would like.

Emma was a breath of exactly the fresh air he needed. He was tired of the old scene. Tired of trying to make something work because he was supposed to, because he had money, because he was expected to be with people like him. Every social gathering he attended ended up being a celebration of people with insane amounts of money and not a speck of joy to be had from it. In the last few weeks, he'd found he'd rather use his money for things that made him happy—like restoring Indigo Pointe—and to do it with people who brought him joy.

"I like roses just fine. Just not three days in a row." Emma handed him half of the tools and grabbed the other half herself. "I'm excited to work on something else tomorrow."

CHAPTER 14

It didn't escape Emma's notice that Theo made closing the door to the cobweb-strung barn look easy, though she struggled with its weight every time. She also noticed the straining of his muscles against his form-fitting cotton shirt, and smiled to herself. It didn't hurt to appreciate these types of things. Call her grateful.

"We're filthy." Theo rubbed his hands on his old jeans.

Emma had seen Theo dressed up at Live Oak Lane, and he'd looked pretty darn hot, but working next to him—joking, chatting, getting to know each other—she decided he was maybe even more attractive in mud-streaked work clothes and a faded cotton T-shirt.

"At least I have a shower." She gave him a smirk and

wiggled her shoulders. "But hey, there might be a rain bucket in the courtyard somewhere."

He laughed, and it was easy to forgive him for that day.

"I might be able to do better than that," he said.

"Then it's a good thing there's soap and water at the office for you."

"It's a good thing there's a matching garçonnière across the courtyard from yours." Theo mimicked her facial expression and body movement, and looked adorable doing it. "You didn't know I stay there sometimes, did you? And I just happen to have soap and water there. Not to mention a towel and fresh clothes."

She tried not to think about it and instead looked at her watch. "Meet me in forty-five minutes? I'm kind of excited for dinner."

"Umm . . . okay?" Theo chuckled.

She'd anticipated the need to explain. "As soon as Zoe heard I've never had gumbo, she said she'd make it for dinner tonight even if it is about ninety degrees out here." Emma was exaggerating the temp, but not by much. And with the oppressive humidity so unlike the dry heat of Eastern Oregon, she thought she just might melt.

They'd reached her cottage, and while Emma unlocked her front door, Theo walked on to his place. She turned just enough to watch him reach his door, unlock it, and walk through. She was getting way too interested in her employer.

Forty-three minutes later, Theo knocked on Emma's door as she was putting away her makeup and other toiletries. She felt infinitely more human than she had an hour ago, now that she'd fixed her hair and put on a flirty summer skirt and cool blouse. Theo, too, had dressed up more than usual. It almost felt like a date.

They started the trek to the office, the late afternoon air still heavy, but the camaraderie between them light and companionable. How much easier it was to be with Theo now that she'd gotten to know him. Just as Zoe had predicted.

"I think I should incorporate a tire swing into the landscaping." Emma's tone was completely serious, but she was kidding. Even though they were cutting through the allée of ancient oaks with their delicious shade, being out of the sun's glare wasn't enough to mitigate the heat.

"A tire swing?" Theo was skeptical, as he should be. She would have been flunked for even suggesting it in a formal, historic garden. Theo brightened with an idea of his own. "How about one of those metal swing sets everyone had in their backyards when we were kids?"

Now she had to recoil. "Ugh. Okay, fine. I get your point." Because it was an eighteenth-century plantation, did everything have to be tight-laced and boring?

Yeah, it did.

"Not a tire swing, and certainly not a swing set, you goof." Emma bumped her shoulder into his arm, causing him to both stumble and smile. "But there's got to be some out-of-the-way live oak tree on the property where we could put up an old-fashioned wooden swing, don't you think?"

She could almost feel the twisted hemp rope in her hands, the wind in her hair, the flip in her stomach as she hurtled forward and back. The romantic in her couldn't help but add a laughing Theo to her daydream.

"We'll see." Theo shook his head as though patronizing a child.

They walked a few more paces in silence until she caught a whiff of dinner.

"Mmm . . ." They were still a parking lot's distance away, but the smell was captivating. Emma breathed in deeply, allowing the deliciousness of the spices to fill her with dreams and optimism. Something grand was coming her way.

"Oh, yeah," Theo agreed, "you're going to love it. Zoe uses fresh crawfish from a farm about a mile down the street. *So* good."

Theo picked up his pace, and Emma hurried to keep up with him. They made it to the office doorstep about the same time Zoe opened the door with a hurried snap.

"Hey, boss. I'm going to take off. Got plans." She seemed out of breath with excitement.

"No problem. Got a date?" Theo asked.

Was Theo hopeful? A second, more alarming idea occurred to Emma—was Theo interested in Zoe? She swallowed the mounting disappointment she had no right to feel.

"Nothing that good. You know my friend Violet who runs the voodoo shop downtown?"

Emma noticed Theo didn't even try to hide his eye roll from her.

"An-y-way." Zoe strung the word out, pointedly ignoring Theo's reaction. "Violet got a new shipment for summer solstice she's excited to share with me. Says they'll impress our visitors."

Theo flicked one of Zoe's earrings that dangled so low it brushed her shoulder. "Like you need any more stuff in our shop to ensnare those poor, unsuspecting tourists." He shook his head. "I almost feel responsible for you leading them astray."

"What?" Zoe acted innocent, but even Emma could see through it. Zoe shrugged. "It's what they come to New Orleans for—voodoo, magic, ghost stories . . ."

"Plantations," Emma offered helpfully, "and history."

"Graveyards and architecture and music . . ." Theo

was way more helpful than Emma had expected him to be.

"It doesn't matter if *I* don't buy into it exactly," Zoe explained. "It's all in fun. I mean, some of my French Creole ancestors believed it, but no one for generations has." She looped the strap of her bag across her chest. "I'm like that gumbo—a little bit of every Louisiana culture in one pot." It was true. Part of what made her so striking was the mix of backgrounds, giving her an exotic look. "It doesn't hurt to take advantage of it."

"Exploit it, you mean." Theo waved her off, chuckling. "Go. Have fun. Just make sure to bring a hoodoo amulet back for our new friend here." He tipped his head toward Emma as if she wouldn't catch on that they were talking about her. "She might need a little protection from all the gnomes around here, and everyone can use a little magic."

With Theo's easy, teasing manner, Emma felt a flush of warmth surge through her chest. She was starting to have an idea what she'd want that magic for.

"Thanks, y'all." Zoe gave both Theo and Emma hugs. "Happy Summer Solstice—the night when wishes come true."

When Zoe flashed her wide, perfect grin at her, Emma couldn't help responding in kind. It was that feeling of home like being back in Oregon.

Fatigued from the hours of work in the sun, Emma

sat across the table from Theo, the simple dinner of gumbo and fresh French bread between them. From the first bite, Emma found herself concentrating on dissecting each individual flavor of the gumbo, allowing the ingredients to pop on her tongue one at a time.

"First impressions of gumbo?" Theo asked, digging in.

"You were right. It's fabulous." She twirled her spoon in her bowl as she tried not to stare at him. Theo looked so good with his hair still the slightest bit damp from his shower. "It was really nice of Zoe to cook for us."

"It's been great not to have to worry where my next meal will come from," Theo conceded, "but the cooking is her idea. She's kicking around the idea of adding a café to Indigo Pointe, and I'm leaving that up to her. Since things have been a little slow around here, she's been trying out recipes."

Emma picked up her spoon and pointed at her bowl. "This is a good one."

Speaking of Zoe, it seemed a little suspicious of her to run off without eating with them. Maybe she was trying to orchestrate something. While she was pleased with the idea, she was uncertain where it might go, so she shifted her thoughts to a safer topic.

"I've been thinking about the grand entrance." Emma spent a lot of time planning it, actually. She wanted it to be perfect. This was the opportunity of a lifetime—what she'd spent years in school dreaming about. That, and she wanted to wow her new employer.

"Want to hear my ideas?"

"Of course."

Emma loved how Theo's eyes lit up. Over the last few days, he'd become so encouraging, so supportive of anything she had to say.

"I'm much better with sketches." She got up from the table and went into the office to scrounge for a sheet of paper, and came back with a pen and a flyer for the Bon Mange Festival in the community a couple of weeks prior. Taking the chair next to Theo rather than her previous one across the table from him, she rearranged the dishes so she could have room.

"When I was online, I saw an aerial view of Indigo Pointe from, I don't know, the forties or fifties, and there was a teardrop-shaped drive from the gate sweeping around the front of the house." As soon as she started talking, their eyes locked and she hadn't been able to look away, despite their closeness. With desire flickering in her chest, she was grateful to have an excuse to look down at the paper, and she began to sketch the outline of the house with the proposed drive, ending with the gate. "The shape makes sense, of course, since there's only one opening."

She waved her pen tip over the entire area. "First,

there is a drainage problem we'll have to address." It was pretty much the entire lawn, but that was okay. The weed-infested grass needed reseeding. "Then we can put in the drive." She started shading the drive again, but looked up in anticipation to what she'd say next. "At the top of the teardrop, what do you think of a flowerbed that mimics the stained-glass rose window in the church?" She swiftly started sketching the details the best she could in the limited space and with only black ink. "The different shades of flowers and landscape rock will create the design."

A circular section emerged from her pen tip at the wide end of the teardrop near the front door. "A person standing next to it might not notice, but from the upstairs gallery, it will be more recognizable." The rightness of it gave her chills. "I think a marble fountain, while not what the original owners ever had, would be a nice addition to the center of the flowerbed."

At her pause, Theo jumped in. "This is amazing, Emma."

Her heart soared at the look of awe on his face. "I'm really looking forward to infusing the property with color—especially blue, given the plantation's name. Speaking of which, do you realize there isn't one surviving indigo plant anywhere?"

Theo looked surprised. "I hadn't thought about it,"

he said, "but being able to point out actual indigo plants would be a nice addition to the tour script." He ran a finger over the stained-glass flowerbed. "It's great."

She couldn't wait to draw out a more detailed sketch so he could get a better idea of her full vision. "I need to figure out the details, materials, that kind of thing."

"We have an account at Contrary Mary's Nursery. Suzette can order whatever you need, and I'll check with her about finding a good crew."

"Hmm . . . on a first-name basis with the proprietor of a local nursery." Emma couldn't keep herself from chuckling. "She wouldn't know anything about garden gnomes, would she?"

Theo seemed to suck in the corners of a smile. "She seems to be quite knowledgeable in many aspects of Louisiana gardening. Certainly a resource, should you find you need some local expertise." He stared eating his gumbo again.

"I see." The fact that Theo made an excuse to look away almost made Emma laugh. She didn't need to have him admit it.

She slid back into her chair across from him to eat a few more bites of dinner, and Theo shifted in his seat, looking up with a new twinkle in his eye. "If you're not too tired after working all day, there's something in the rose garden I want to show you." A cautious excitement in Theo's voice caught Emma off guard.

"And it is . . ." She waited for him to fill in the blank.

"A surprise." He looked pleased with himself. She'd walked into his trap, but how could she not?

"Is it another gnome?" She narrowed her eyes at him. The gnomes were cute, and she enjoyed the unexpectedness of them, but she didn't want to get her hopes up for something exciting if that was all it was.

Theo shook his head, mischievousness in his expression. "Not telling."

"A plant?"

He shook his head again.

"I like the way you 'don't tell.'" Emma took her last bite, savoring the spicy Cajun seasoning before throwing out another guess. This one hopeful. "A lead for my family mystery?"

The guy couldn't hold a secret in two hands. His face told her everything.

"I can't believe you didn't tell me earlier!" She wanted to whack him, but settled for a playful glare.

"I couldn't! I was too hungry." He took another bite as if to prove it.

"You better eat fast, then, mister, or I'll take off without you." It wasn't like she actually could, considering she had no idea what it was or where she would find it. Her heartbeat quickened in anticipation.

Theo responded by obediently gulping his last bites of gumbo, swiping his French bread through the bowl to mop up the rest, and shoving it all into his mouth. Emma rolled her eyes. So much for manners, but she appreciated how he matched her excitement with his own.

They rinsed their bowls and loaded them in the dishwasher, stowed the leftovers in the fridge for the next day's lunch, and headed toward the churchyard.

"Spill it." Emma poked him in the ribs as they walked side by side. "What did you see?"

"An ivy pattern in the metalwork." The air shimmered around them in the approaching sunset.

"Seriously? Where? How did I miss that? Is it the same as the one I saw upstairs? I mean, I guess it probably is if you're telling me about it—"

"Take a breath," he teased.

Theo chuckled and Emma realized she had, indeed, been asking too many questions too quickly. She exhaled long and slow, but it was now her turn to pick up the pace.

CHAPTER 15

"Over here." Theo was pleased to have discovered something to share with Emma. If only they could figure out if the randomness of the ivy motif actually meant something. There had to be a pattern, a reason, a key to figuring out the anomalies.

In all the pruning, fertilizing, and "training," as Emma referred to it, they'd been winding rose branches around a simple fence that ran the length of the old church. All of the iron posts had been unadorned, except for one. On the fourth post from the north end, he'd felt a design under his leather-gloved fingertips. Knowing Emma would want to see it, he'd held on to this nugget of information until just the right time—which he hoped was now.

"What do you think?" he asked, giving her a chance to examine the design.

He waited patiently, noticing the crickets' chirping in the background. Theo watched Emma, captivated by her graceful movements. Her slender frame bent to study the design, the soft skin of her arched neck pale despite her time in the sun. She pushed a lock of hair behind her ear, something he'd noticed she did frequently. The motion was endearing in its normalcy. Emma was completely comfortable with herself, unaware of how beautiful she was, and that was more attractive than anything else.

"I think it matches." She crouched in front of the post, but looked up at him with those hazel eyes wide with question. "Why here?"

He spread his hands helplessly. With no answer or guess, he allowed the words to float on the air.

"It has to mean something." She stood and crossed her arms over her chest. "The church." She dropped her arms and ran to him, grasping both of his hands. He couldn't breathe for listening to her, feeling her excitement telegraphed through her trembling fingers. "Can we go inside the church? I bet there's more; there has to be."

Theo gave her a weak smile. He would give her anything, but this . . . this would be a disappointment. "Sure, but I have to warn you. It's a mess inside—

completely awful. Even if there was something at one time, I doubt there's anything left to find." She started to object, but he stopped her. "Let's take a look."

The three concrete steps leading to the front door of the church were cracked and crumbling. Fishing the key ring from his pocket, Theo located the correct one and forced the stiff tumblers inside the lock to move. Opening both wooden doors wide released a potpourri of horrible smells: stale air, acrid wood ash, and the dank hint of mold. Theo gave it a few seconds to air out before taking a deep breath and heading for the bank of side windows, eager to open them wide. The trapped air vented through the windows like steam from a pressure cooker.

"Oh." Emma stood, looking disappointed on the doorstep.

"Could you catch the light switch to your right?"

Emma would have been expecting more and he should have prepared her. But seeing it was the only way to truly take it in.

At some point in the last century, someone had removed all of the church pews from the open sanctuary and had laid some clunky, off-white ceramic tile, stripping the character from the building. In a few places, drywall had been nailed to studs, but the handyman hadn't made much progress before abandoning the project, leaving it a strange mash-up of nineteenth-century charred church and twentieth-century horrible handyman. It wasn't even clear what the renovation plans had been.

Emma flicked on the temporary bulbs that barely illuminated the space and took a few tentative steps to Theo's side. "I guess I don't have to ask what happened here." She slowly took in the room—probably looking for metalwork. "My great-grandfather's journal mentioned a church fire in his journal, but sort of in passing, as if he expected everyone to know what happened. Do you know any of the details?"

"I don't know for sure. I think it was near the end of the Civil War." He recalled tidbits in the research he'd done on the place, but not much. "I don't know if it pertains to your mystery, but it would be interesting to find out more." He fell into step beside her as she surveyed the room.

"The good news is, it won't take long to see everything," she joked.

"The bad news is that there's nothing to see," he quipped back.

"Your optimism is astounding."

And her sarcasm was spot-on. Her quick-wittedness was one of the many things that attracted him.

Emma halted in the center of the room near the front where the preacher's lectern would have been, but instead of looking down for markings on the floor, she looked toward the stained-glass window that would have lit up the room behind the speaker. Weakening sunlight fought its way through the colorful glass, illuminating it enough that it glowed. "The colors are so much more vibrant from the inside."

"We're really lucky the window survived." He looked to the east where a few of the arched gothic windows had once been, but had since been boarded up with plywood, splitting and engorged with decades of sunshine and rainwater. "It alone is worth renovating the building."

After getting their fill of the rose window, they took a few more careful steps around the perimeter, finding nothing of value. Emma stopped at one of the arched windows on the side opposite the rose garden. A bramble of blackberry bushes with fruit that wasn't yet ripe encroached toward the windows. "Why is it there's no cemetery on the property?"

Theo's mind scrambled for a plausible explanation. How had he never wondered that himself? "Perhaps it has something to do with the high water table and all that? You know, the reason there are all those mausoleums around New Orleans."

"Yes, but all the way out here? It doesn't make sense that people in 1790 would take their loved ones miles and miles away from home when their church was here."

"True." There must be something closer.

"Do you think there's a cemetery somewhere else on the plantation?" she asked.

"I don't remember one, but it's possible. I haven't actually walked the entire property. I wasn't allowed to just wander as a kid since the place didn't belong to us." Instead of allowing him to roam, his uncle had always put him to work when he'd come, which hadn't been so bad, as he'd been reminded working with the roses that day.

Emma raised her fingers to touch the window molding and then glanced at him. "I'll keep an eye out while I work."

"On second thought, maybe we shouldn't," Theo joked, making his eyes cartoonishly wide. "We wouldn't want to disturb the ghosts. We just might be the only plantation in the area that doesn't claim to be haunted."

"Being haunted is 'in.'"

"True. Would help with marketing." It was a joke, of course. He'd never noticed anything otherworldly and wouldn't make something up to draw in visitors. "Oh. You know what? There's a cemetery down the road a bit. Maybe it was a community one."

Examining every nook and cranny of the gutted church didn't take long. The hinges and door handles were the same boring hardware used most everywhere else, and they could find no other metalwork. Theo even examined the charred woodwork in case a similar ivy motif was carved there, but it wasn't.

"I think we're out of luck." That he was disappointed hardly made sense. This was Emma's quest, not his, yet if the treasure was on his property and the Lamberts felt claim to it . . . He didn't want to think about it coming between the two of them. Money maybe didn't mean much to him, but family and history did.

Emma let out a loud breath. "I don't know what else to do or where to look. Do you think a local historical library or something?"

"It's certainly the next step since we haven't seen anything else around here. At least we could find out more about this fire. When do you think you'll have a day off from trees and roses?"

"Oh, Theo!" Emma abandoned his side and rushed to stand in front of the horribly dirty windows overlooking the rose garden. A look of awe dawned on her delicate features. The last of the day's sunlight was slipping into twilight. Only a tinge of lavender remained, seeping into the indigo color of night.

Though he wanted to wrap his arms around her from behind, cradling her to his chest so they could both watch the fading of the light, he said, "Let's go outside where we can see it better." He touched her arm, and she took his hand, accompanying him out the door.

Almost immediately Emma gasped and dropped Theo's hand. She ran through the arbor to the maze of hedges, hurrying toward something other than the vanishing sunset.

"Are those—" She ran to the bush and scooped a speck of light into her hands, cupping the other over the top. "Fireflies!"

Her childlike excitement brought back snatches of memories—long-ago summer evenings spent catching lightning bugs with his cousins. A telltale blink in the bush near Emma caught his eye, and Theo scrambled to beat her to it. "Got one."

"I've never seen them in real life before." Emma looked down at her clasped hands, lifting the top one enough to see the light blink again before the insect crawled out and took flight. "Shoot. It escaped."

"They tend to do that." He remembered losing way too many that way, but then again, it made for opportunities to catch more. "Over there!" He pointed to their left.

She dove to the side, but then twirled mid-air, focusing instead near his shoulder. "There's one behind you."

Theo turned out of her way, but he saw it evade her once again, this time landing on her head. "Here." He laughed as he gently guided it from her hair into his hand.

"You've got one too." She reached behind his shoulder but froze, calling attention to the fact that they were inches apart, their arms around each other.

Realizing for the first time how much taller he was than Emma, Theo leaned down to whisper near her ear, "All we need is a little music."

His head whirled in a frenzy of joy in her presence. He'd abandoned chasing lightning bugs decades ago; it had never been this fun. But as entertaining as it was, having her in his arms was even better.

"Music?" She looked up at him with wide, trusting eyes.

Emma hadn't stepped back, and Theo took that as a good sign. The rising moon highlighted the freckles sprinkled like fairy dust across the bridge of her nose.

"Aren't we dancing?" He put a hand to the small of her back and guided her gently, slowly toward him, never looking away from her sweet, hazel eyes.

Her smile melted him as she dropped a hand to his bicep and held out her other. "Is that what we're doing?"

He led her through a few twirls, trying his darnedest to think of a few notes of a waltz but ended up instead with the Beatles, singing about places he remembered that had changed. Like the Indigo Pointe of his childhood. He sang softly into the crown of her head, more so there would be music than to convey any particular purpose as he moved her through the maze of hedges. As much as he wanted to restore and protect the plantation, he was starting to realize that, just like the song, it was having Emma in his life that he cared most about. When he could no longer remember the words, he resorted to humming, allowing his movements to slow into a sway. She looked so happy in his arms and he felt content, more at home with her here at Indigo than he'd ever been anywhere with anyone else.

He placed her hand on his chest and tucked that glorious lock of hair behind her ear. How many times he'd watched her do that and wanted to do it himself. Allowing his fingertips to brush her jawline, he dropped his chin slowly, giving her plenty of time to pull back. Instead, she met him halfway. Their kiss was hesitant at first, lips and breath mingling softly, but became more sure.

He allowed his eyes to close, enjoying the two of them surrounded by the allure of lightning bugs, kissing to the music of crickets, accompanied only by a breeze ruffling through tree leaves. Summer solstice at Indigo Pointe was indeed magical.

CHAPTER 16

"How's it going?" Zoe lobbed the words like a volleyball across the allée of trees as she approached Emma mid-morning.

"Hey, Zoe. Out for a stroll?"

Zoe nodded. "I needed a quick walk and a breath of air."

Emma could understand that. After growing up on a farm, she was pretty sure she'd have trouble with office work every day. "That gumbo last night was a-maz-ing." Emma knew she was gushing, but after her perfect evening with Theo, everything made her overly happy. She tried to rein it in by bending down to sift through the few leaves under the worst of the stricken live oaks. There wasn't much. The hired lawn crew had done a good job cleaning up when they'd trimmed.

"Are they going to survive?" Zoe sounded just as worried as she'd been waiting for the arborist when Emma first met her.

"Oh, yes." Emma wanted to alleviate any lingering doubt Zoe harbored. "Lots of late-winter rain this year?"

"You could say that," Zoe scoffed. "Record-breaking flooding, February or March, which is saying something for Louisiana. It didn't seem to affect the sugarcane, thankfully, but I had no idea the water would hurt the trees." Zoe stood with her palms pressed to her chest as if losing one of the trees would break her heart. Emma didn't blame her. It would break her heart too.

"All we have to do now is spray some fungicide, and they'll be fine." Emma touched one of the cupped, deformed leaves that would stay until the next set of leaves pushed it off in March. "They'll be deformed until next year, but we won't lose any more either. I doubt the guests will notice."

"You're probably right." Zoe ran her fingers along the rough bark of the trunk, looking up through the canopy. Maybe looking for her squirrel friends. "Were there any gnomes this morning?"

"Only one." But its perfectness made Emma's heart squeeze with pleasure. Theo was so observant. Who said guys didn't listen? It was almost as though Theo had seen her daydream of him pushing her on a wooden swing, the breeze blowing through her hair. Except that he couldn't have.

"And?" Zoe prompted.

"It's the cutest little gnome couple sharing a wood swing." She'd discovered it in an overgrown crepe myrtle between the garçonnière and the outdoor kitchen. "They're adorable."

"Oh, really?" Zoe raised her eyebrows. "Had a good time last night, did you?"

Emma willed herself not to react, but at the memory of those sweet kisses, her cheeks grew hot. "I told you the gumbo was great."

"Uh-huh." Zoe was smarter than that. Heck, a five-year-old was smarter than that.

"The sunset was gorgeous. Oh, and fireflies! We chased fireflies." That was definitely her second-favorite part of the evening, pushing the gumbo to a solid third. "I'd never seen them in real life before."

"Yeah." It was obvious Zoe wasn't buying that something else hadn't happened. Emma almost shrugged. Let Zoe wonder.

Zoe continued, "I did tell you that summer solstice at Indigo Pointe would be magical. I bet you had a wish granted, too. Didn't you?"

The kisses probably qualified, though Emma was

disappointed that the search of the charred chapel hadn't produced any new clues. Still, finding the metalwork in the rose garden was a step forward, even if she didn't know what it meant or how to tie it to her family history yet. "I think I might have."

Trying to get her mind off the evening before and onto work, Emma considered what to do next. A project that didn't require a lot of bending would be a welcome relief. Maybe trimming the crepe myrtles, including the one with the gnome swing.

"I do have to say, this is the happiest I've seen Theo in . . . well, ever," Zoe said.

Emma hadn't thought her smile could get any larger, but she felt her heart swell even more.

"I mean, I did see him get all excited about ten-cent cheeseburgers at McDonald's that one random Thursday night over Christmas break junior year. He must have eaten a dozen." Zoe messed with the bangles on her arm, drawing them up toward her elbow and then releasing them to settle with a tinkle around her wrist. "Which is ridiculous on so many levels, especially for him, but that's nothing to the way he lights up around you."

Emma giggled, feeling very much like she was in high school again herself. "I guess it's good that I make him happier than ten-cent cheeseburgers."

Zoe watched a car drive by and checked her phone. "Even though we don't have any tours scheduled today, I probably ought to head back into the office. A quiet day is just what the doctor ordered to get the books in order." She shook her head. "I knew managing Indigo Pointe would be a big job, but I had no idea how hard the previous owner tried to bury the place. There's so much we need to do to get it back in the black."

Emma and Theo had had that discussion the day before while they worked. "Theo said he couldn't have hired a more business-savvy accountant and all-around managing guru than you," she said. "His words, not mine."

Now it was Zoe's turn to grin like a schoolgirl. "Speaking of Theo." Zoe tipped her head, pointing to Emma's side. "I hear he has special lunch plans for the two of you." Sure enough, Theo walked up behind her, basket in hand. Zoe touched Emma's arm. "See you later."

"So . . ." Emma said as Theo came closer. He was attractive, to say the least—a great build, good sense of style, handsome features—but as she got to know him, she found there was even more to like about him.

"So . . ." Theo stopped right in front of her, the toes of his shoes almost touching hers, a reminder of last night's dance. He had the most amazing voice, and she could have danced with him all night. His blue eyes searched her face, and after several seconds, he smiled. "Could I interest you in a picnic?"

The way his eyes had examined her, Emma reciprocated in earnest. There was something almost vulnerable in his question, and she found it sweet. She reached for his hand and threaded her fingers through his. "It's a little early for lunch," she teased.

"I didn't say we'd eat right away."

"Well," Emma hedged, though she was more than willing to comply. "If you think it's okay with my boss . . ."

In true nineteenth-century fashion, he offered her his elbow and she took it. She followed his lead as he started strolling across the back of the property. "Oh, I think he'll be fine with it."

"I meant Zoe." She couldn't resist.

"Ahem." Theo cleared his throat. "Zoe may be the manager, but as *her* boss, you still answer to me."

Emma laughed and squeezed his forearm. "I know."

Theo had such a dry delivery, half the time she didn't know if he was being serious—until she saw that mischievous look on his face.

He paused at the animal pen, drawing an apple from the basket. Moments later, the curious horse ambled up to claim it.

"How are you today, Phillippe?" Theo allowed the

horse to nuzzle into his palm when grabbing the fruit. He patted the side of the horse's neck, and after the horse finished his snack, Theo and Emma started their stroll again.

"Where are we going? And don't you dare say it's a surprise."

"Well, it is," he quipped. He led her into a copse of trees at the back corner of the property behind the barn and secluded from everything else. "I was looking for the right tree for our swing."

Emma's heart fluttered at the admission, and she eyed the trees, looking for one old enough and with enough open space for the honor.

"And then I found this." Theo brought her to a small rectangle of wrought iron fence, probably eighteen inches high and almost invisible under a tangle of weeds and vines.

"The cemetery?" Emma couldn't believe it.

"The cemetery." Theo set the basket down and stepped over the fence.

Patches of weeds and clumps of yellow-blossomed wildflowers covered almost everything, but as they moved the vegetation aside, stone grave markers dotted the rectangle like spots on a domino. Theo and Emma worked until each of the stones had been revealed.

"I can't believe how many of these markers have

1865 as the death year," Emma said after she'd uncovered the third one. "Are you seeing the same thing?"

"I noticed that." Theo stood, arching his back and then started to work again. "Maybe a smallpox or cholera outbreak?" He dropped some weeds onto the pile Emma had started.

"Or . . ." In her heart, she knew she was right. "The church fire."

They picked their way carefully through the plot, taking careful note of the dates.

"Not just 1865, Theo." Emma stopped in front of a matching pair of headstones. "March 26, 1865."

Rosemund Heidel, May 3, 1833–March 26, 1865 sat snugly next to *Gen. Bradish Heidel, Nov. 24, 1823–March 26, 1865.*

Theo exhaled slowly, pausing before speaking. "Do you recognize those names, Emma?"

Her eyes flicked to his face. "I probably should, shouldn't I?"

He swallowed. "He owned Indigo Pointe during the Civil War."

"Oh." Emma stood like a statue, unable to move. "Then I'm related to them?" Until Opa had shared his story a few months ago, Emma hadn't spent much time studying her family tree. She knew she ought to at least recognize surnames. Family shouldn't be strangers.

Theo tugged his phone from his pocket and snapped a few frames of the headstones.

"Wait." Emma put both fists on her hips to show Theo she meant business, although she was teasing. "Do you want to explain why it's okay for you to take photos of my family's gravestones but not okay for me to take pictures inside the house?" She raised her eyebrows high, waiting for an answer.

"Um . . ." Theo looked appropriately chagrined. "I'm kind of embarrassed to admit it, but it has everything to do with Indigo Pointe's online image and future marketing." He raked a hand through his hair. "Honestly, I should probably be more worried about people posting pictures of the exterior, since it needs so much work."

Emma tried not to get annoyed, considering she was doing her best to wrangle overgrown vegetation.

Theo continued, "I plan to have the interior cleaned up as well, so I didn't want less-than-flattering photos to tarnish Indigo Pointe's reputation."

Emma scoffed, but before she could say anything, Theo followed it up with, "I know, it makes absolutely no sense, and I'm sorry I was such a jerk about it."

Emma stepped toward him, catching his hand in hers before she kissed him on his sandpapery cheek. "You're forgiven." She looked down at his phone and back up into his eyes. "So the grave markers?"

"Easier than writing down all the info."

He was cute *and* smart. "Good idea."

To help get clear shots, Emma walked past each marker, pulling out clumps of crabgrass to reveal the writing. When she had uncovered them all, Emma stood back for Theo to finish capturing each with his phone. She was about to turn away when Emma caught a glimmer of light off to one side. It reminded her of how she found Indigo Pointe in the first place.

She took a few steps to where she thought it had been, but couldn't find anything reflective. "Did you, um . . ." She didn't want to sound crazy and almost decided not to ask when the air sparkled again, this time right in front of her. "Did—do you see that?"

"See what?"

As Theo picked his way toward her, over a few headstones, Emma felt around with her fingertips under the ground cover, hoping any snakes were long gone. Her fingertips met with the smooth coldness of another stone. She began ripping away the variegated leaves, ceasing movement when she revealed the familiar ivy imprint.

"Theo, look!"

He hurried over, as excited as she was. This was the only grave decorated with the ivy logo so far. The top line simply read *Treager*. How sad that there wasn't a first name. Underneath were the dates *1862–1925*.

"Another clue?" he asked, as if she knew more than he did.

"Maybe." She shrugged her shoulders. "The dates don't match the others. And we still don't have any idea what this ivy thing is all about. It may mean nothing."

"Or it may mean everything." How comforting it was that Theo was on her side. That he didn't think she was nuts for wanting to figure out the mystery. "It's worth looking into."

When they'd documented every marker, Theo picked up the basket and they walked to the other side of the small grove. Even more secluded than the cemetery, this spot had a lone live oak on a slight rise overlooking fields of sugarcane. A thick quilt was spread on the soft grass in the tree's shade.

"This is perfect," Emma whispered, not wanting to break the silence. The quiet beauty of the clearing made it not only a great picnic spot, but the large live oak had a branch exactly the right height and girth. "I can't picture a better place for a swing."

They sat on the quilt, their backs to the tree.

"Not even in a crepe myrtle?" Theo asked.

"A-ha! You *are* the one placing the gnomes!" An admission of guilt if she'd ever heard one.

He shook his head. "I'm pretty sure they do it themselves." Theo unloaded fresh croissants, juicy strawberries, and cubes of cheese as he spoke. "Indigo Pointe is enchanted."

"I see." She took the bottle of water he offered. "Curiously, the gnomes always seem to know what our conversations have been." She leaned forward, whispering conspiratorially. "I think they've been spying on us."

"Is that so?"

CHAPTER 17

Theo had had such a great time with Emma over the past few days, he couldn't get her out of his mind. As he'd watched her work her magic on the landscape, she'd cast a spell over him. There was no other explanation as to why he would allow her to tutor him in the art of plant care.

Ever since Emma had persuaded him to explore the church, it was as if the two of them had emerged into a world all their own. A place where it felt right to dance amid lightning bugs and picnic on the brink of history. And every day he spent with her helped him realize there wasn't anything he didn't like about this amazing woman or any place he didn't want to be with her. The joy he found in being with her flowed into other aspects of his life. She made him want to be better, to mend fences."

He scrolled to the correct contact and pushed the button to initiate a call.

"Good afternoon, Don. This is Theo Lambert." He'd made scores of uncomfortable calls, but he couldn't think he'd done quite this before. "If you have a minute, I'd like to chat with you about the other day." The former tour guide for Indigo Pointe hadn't hung up on him yet, so Theo took that as a good sign. "I believe I need to offer an apology for not listening to your side of things the other day."

Theo shuffled papers on his desk at his New Orleans home. He'd gotten caught up with things over the past few days despite spending as much time with Emma as he could. He was able to work more efficiently now that he had motivation in the form of someone he wanted to spend time with.

He finished his call with Don, and then he moved on to finishing what he couldn't delegate to his assistant Antonio. Once that was done, he was able to free up a day later in the week. While the break wouldn't be forever, Theo had earned some time to do something he wanted to do and remember what it was like to have a little fun.

Theo was falling for Emma—dear, sweet Emma Treager—his family nemesis, his employee, the one who helped him find joy in the simple things in life. Like fireflies and garden gnomes.

Today he had new plans. Traitorous plans, his father would have called them if he knew. Plans that did not involve working in the gardens, but helping her solve her family mystery instead.

Zoe was in the parking lot when Theo pulled in.

"Hey, boss." Zoe looked up from sweeping the front walk.

"Thanks for the gumbo the other night." His gratitude was rather belated, so he moved on quickly. "Get anything interesting from Violet?" She would have been expecting him to ask about the hoodoo trinkets she loved to trifle with.

"A few scarves and amulets." Zoe pursed her lips and eyed him as if assessing his mood. "What do you think about stocking voodoo dolls?"

Theo pulled a face and shook his head. "I'd rather not."

Zoe chuckled. "I figured, but you've been in such a good mood lately, I thought I'd try." She hugged the broom handle to her chest, folding her arms around it, and leaned against the building. "And how was *your* summer solstice? I heard it went rather well."

The well-placed emphasis communicated that she knew, or at least knew a little of what had gone on that night. "Did you see Emma's design for the entrance?"

"Fine, don't tell me." She wiggled her eyebrows at him, but then got serious. "Anything special on the docket today?"

"For me or you?"

Zoe laughed. "Me. I already know what you'll be up to, and somehow, some way, it involves that girl you follow around like a puppy dog."

Busted. "An adorable puppy dog, though, right?" The woman knew him way too well. Good friends were gold.

She nodded. "You kids have fun together."

"One thing." Theo had almost forgotten to tell her. "You said our new tour guide has limited hours around school, so I made a call, and I wanted to let you know that Don's back if you'll go ahead and put him on the schedule as well."

Zoe gave him an appraising look, and he knew he'd not only surprised her, but done the right thing. "That's good. We're actually going to be a bit busier today."

Zoe floated into the office, and Theo stepped back to his truck, flooded with a feeling of contentment. Sandwiched between his best friend and his new love interest, everything was going great for him. Before heading to Emma's, he needed to hide his gnomes for the day, and this one was going to be fun—Emma had given the best lead-in so far.

He pulled the gnome from the box on his back seat,

unwound the protective bubble wrap, and situated it in the bushes beside his pickup to be discovered later. Not unlike the ivy-stamped metalwork amid the rest of the wrought iron fence. Well, okay, maybe gnomes weren't quite as subtle.

Theo stuck his hands into his pockets, strolling toward Emma's garçonnière. Indigo Pointe already looked so much better, and Emma had only been working on the landscaping for a short time. So far, much of it had been taming and cleaning up overgrowth the previous owner had permitted, but Emma was also starting to make forward progress as well. The designs she'd shown him for the front entrance were phenomenal. Far better than he had pictured. He was thrilled that he'd hired the exact right person for the job, but he knew it had more to do with luck and timing.

He was even more gratified that she'd fallen into his life, yet he couldn't help wondering, again, exactly what the nature of the dispute between the Treagers and the Lamberts was. Why would they both claim the treasure? What was worth fighting over? Perhaps he and Emma would discover it when doing their research today.

Theo hoped whatever it was wouldn't push Emma away from him. She didn't seem like the kind of person who would allow an old family feud to taint their relationship, not when she'd known nothing about it before. Hopefully as she learned more, it wouldn't put a rift between them, even if it ended up being something that absolutely had to stay with Indigo Pointe. Would she blame him for keeping it from her family? And which did he care about more now—the ownership and preservation of the plantation, or his budding relationship with the most amazing woman he'd ever met?

Arriving at the cottage before Emma emerged for the day, Theo settled himself on the porch's top step. He leaned his forearms across his knees and stared down the brick path to his cottage. His eyes followed the soft moss that grew between the bricks; the once-shaggy hedges that lined the brick path were now trimmed into crisp lines. The overall effect of the formal garden from the upstairs window had always been breathtaking, but with Emma's loving care, it had become the bright jewel of the property. Website hits had doubled in the past two weeks alone, and he attributed it to Instagram and Facebook posts from pleased guests, Emma's handiwork, and the new tour guide, Maurice.

When the door behind him creaked open, Theo didn't say a word but simply leaned back against the porch post, allowing today's gnomes, two tough-looking gnomes in leather bomber jackets and combat boots, to do the speaking for him. One chubby guy was kicked back in a hammock suspended between two resin stumps, and the other held a picket sign that read *On Strike*.

"My helpers are looking rather lazy today." Emma's voice floated like a summer scent on the breeze—light and happy.

She plopped down on the step next to him and muscled him with a stare. Unable to look away, Theo threw his hands into the air. "If they're not working in the gardens, neither should you."

"And what do you suggest instead?"

"I have an idea." He gave Emma his best smoldering look with a hint of a smile. Or at least he hoped it came off that way. He wanted her to think about sharing another kiss or two—or ten—but he really had something completely different in mind. For now. "I thought today might be a good day for research at the historical library. See what we can find out about the Treagers, Indigo Pointe, and the church fire. You game?"

"I was hoping you'd say that."

The excitement on her face made him happier than his morning cup of protein shake. Not that it took much to do that, but still, he knew he'd chosen the day's plans well.

"Mind if I change?" She looked down at her clothes, which, while they fit her well and she looked as beautiful as ever, were admittedly all wrong for the day. Her cheeks colored again, as if she needed to be embarrassed for wearing gardening clothes for work.

The woman blushed way too easily, but he liked that she couldn't hide anything, including her emotions. "Of course." He made a show of looking at his blank wrist. "We've got all the time in the world."

He watched as Emma turned back to her door. There was something so light, so right, about her, and he knew he could spend a lifetime admiring her.

He shook his head. Wow, he was getting sappy for someone the community considered to be a beast. If his business associates knew how soft he was getting, he'd be wickedly taken advantage of.

It wasn't long before Emma stepped from her cottage completely transformed. She looked resplendent in a blue and white sundress, her hair cascading in loose waves across her shoulders, the deep brunette setting off her porcelain skin. Even when she caught him staring, he didn't look away.

She smiled briefly, but then a serious look settled on her features. "Theo, I'm afraid I've been thinking about that gnome on strike."

"That could be dangerous." Theo matched her grave tone.

"I know."

They started walking toward his pickup back at the office lot. Their hands bumped, and he grabbed hold, squeezing slightly, so she would know it was intentional.

"He must be protesting something."

Theo hadn't thought that one through all the way. "You did call him and his friends lazy. Employees don't take to being treated so poorly."

She laughed, and he tried to hold on to the sound, to memorize it so he could hear it as he fell asleep that night. "You may have a point. No one wants to feel underappreciated."

Did she feel he didn't appreciate her? He chanced a look, but didn't find an answer. "Would you feel I'm being insincere if I told you your plans for the main entrance are inspired?" He hoped she knew he really meant it. "Since you showed me, I've spent some time online looking at other plantations, and I feel your designs are creative and elegant and, well, perfect." He swallowed, allowing the rest of his thought to come out as a whisper he almost hoped she wouldn't hear, "Just as you are."

They were almost to his pickup when Emma noticed the last gnome of the day. She dropped his hand and sprinted to the little guy. "Is that . . . ?" She crouched to inspect him, standing to face Theo when he caught up with her. "A gnome with a camera?"

"What? A paparazzo gnome hiding in the bushes?" He tried to sound shocked, but quickly had to camouflage his mirth. He opened the door for her. "At least now we know how they've overheard so many of our private conversations." He raised an eyebrow.

Before he could close the door, she leaned forward and gave him a quick peck on the lips. He sure liked this woman.

CHAPTER 18

Already familiar with the public narrative about Indigo Pointe, the only place Theo could think of to learn more was the local public library. Emails and phone calls to the local historical society had gone unanswered, and their Facebook page hadn't been updated in six months, but he hoped that by going in person, they could find a librarian who would be able to point them in the right direction.

But he'd been wrong. The genealogy section of small Nouvelle Foix Library was stuffed into a windowless conference room, two tables ringed with bookshelves. While there was a desk for a librarian, the chair was empty, and a half-full mug of coffee waited beside a hibernating computer. He assumed that pointed to a temporary absence, but after half an hour, no one had reappeared.

The only other person in the room was an elderly woman, curled like a comma around a corner of the table. She looked far more comfortable in her sleep than the hard edge of a table should afford.

Absent any guidance, Theo and Emma perused the room, finding only four books that looked promising enough to snatch off the shelves. In a room full of books with everything from family crests and tartan patterns to maps of faraway townships, there wasn't much else other than actual books of genealogy, which would be more searchable online.

He and Emma spread out on the unoccupied table, Emma cracking open the first dusty tome before he'd even pulled out his tablet computer and logged on. The room was dim, the air musty, and Theo tried hard to concentrate on his screen rather than the lack of light and suffocating dust. If he needed something beautiful to look at, she was right there in front of him.

"I'm glad the original documents are typed out for me," Emma whispered, pointing at a black-and-white photo of a handwritten ledger. The writing was neat and uniform, but also flat and thin, almost to the point of being indistinguishable.

"It's hard enough to understand what they're talking about without having to decipher it in the first place." Emma kept her voice quiet, obviously in deference to the sleeping woman, whose mouth sagged open, her breath whistling when she inhaled. The dust must have been bothering her as well.

Emma looked longingly at Theo's computer and he pulled it to his chest, protecting it in case she was thinking of negotiating a trade.

"Now you know why I gave you *that* job." He looked down at the note he'd started. When he was ready, he would right-click and the computer program would convert his handwriting into type. The irony of Emma's complaint wasn't lost on him.

He already had a couple of internet tabs open—one with Family Search to track down the first name of the Treager from the gravestone, another to search archived newspapers from the Library of Congress.

"Are you finding anything?" Emma interrupted his searching.

Theo laughed. "Give me a chance; I just got started."

"Every internet search I did at home was useless. And so are these." She patted the stack of books. "Don't get me wrong. I love books." She looked around her, her eyes sweeping every volume on the shelves. "Are you a reader, Theo?"

He scanned the top hits, looking for something more than he already knew. "I haven't had a lot of time since I graduated college, but I listen to my fair share of nonfiction audiobooks." It helped him fall asleep when he was recovering from jet lag.

She gave him a look of *Really?*

"What?" he asked. She was probably someone who read the classics for fun, and he had a sudden desire to pull out some of his favorites, like maybe a King Arthur tale.

"Fiction's where it's at—there's no better escape."

"Escape?" What was she trying to leave?

"It's like traveling, only never leaving home."

"Leaving home is the point of traveling." He loved debating with her. Behind her witty quips was an intelligence and appreciation for the world and people that he admired. "How will you ever see the gardens at Vigeland Park in Norway if you never leave home?"

"Some people use their imaginations, Theo." She smirked at him. "And Google images."

"Reading's great, but you'll like it better in person." He shook his head at her. "Let's get back to work, smarty pants."

She couldn't actually mean that she didn't want to travel. And if she was impressed with this dingy library, she would love the opulence of his collection in New Orleans. Theo opened his mouth to tell her about it, but changed his mind. He'd show her in person so he could see her expression when she walked through the door. Saturday. He'd ask her on a real date for Saturday, take her out for some classic Cajun cuisine, and then surprise her with the library.

She'd finished with the first book and pulled another toward her.

"I was a history undergrad," Theo explained, "so I learned some nifty research tricks." Not that he put them to use very often. There wasn't much need for it in real estate investing or wills and trusts, and if there was, usually his assistants did the legwork.

He changed his internet search to *fire + Indigo Pointe*, but no relevant hits surfaced. He considered how he might need to alter his keywords. "I've missed this." It was like a puzzle.

"I bet your search is going faster." Emma didn't look too happy. He watched her scan through the index and then fan the pages to the correct location. Her finger traced the book, marking her progress as she skimmed. When she didn't find what she wanted, she pursed her lips to one side for about two seconds and then went to the index again for another entry. "At least yours has a digital search."

He smiled at her, completely forgetting he was supposed to be doing half of the work. "You're the one who said you couldn't find anything online."

"Well, did you?" Her look challenged him.

"Yes, and no." He kept focused on the computer, not ready to share anything quite yet. "Still working on it."

In his periphery he saw that she closed the second book and hesitantly pulled another toward her, opening the pages as if afraid what might be on them. As she read, her shoulders slumped and creases formed between her eyebrows. A sadness pulled about the corners of her mouth, her eyes shiny with unspoken emotion.

"Emma?" When she lifted her eyes, all he saw was pain. "What did you find?"

She swallowed hard, and instead of answering, turned the book for him to see. Each page had a date with names, ages, and descriptions, followed by a dollar amount. A record of sales at another plantation within the same parish as Indigo Pointe.

His throat froze and a lump formed like a glacier in his stomach. He closed his eyes against the sight.

Intellectually, he understood that neither he nor Emma could choose where they came from or who their ancestors were, but it didn't soften the blow.

Desperate to pull her from the emotional descent he saw her spiraling into, Theo vowed to find something positive about the next article he found. He flipped through a string of photos until one caught his eye. Clicking on the black-and-white image, he saw two women, probably in their fifties or sixties, their skin contrasting each other's, standing shoulder to shoulder. Each woman had what looked like a son or daughter and a grandson at their sides. The young boys, around six or seven years old, sat playing in the dirt, forever frozen in a giggle. "Pruning the Lambert Rose." It was the caption that snagged his attention. Theo scrutinized the building behind them.

"This is the church on Indigo Pointe, isn't it?" Theo turned the computer to face Emma.

As she closed her book, a tear leaked out of the corner of her eye, but Theo pretended not to notice as she brushed it away. After a long moment of examining the photo, Emma spoke, a false cheer in her voice.

"It has to be, and it matches what your parents said about the roses. After all these years, it still looks the same." She picked the computer up and walked around the table. Taking the seat next to him, she replaced the computer where they could both see. "I think the picture was taken in the twenties, don't you think? Look at the woman's hair."

He nodded. "Sometime around that, I would think."

Emma tried to enlarge the photo, but it was at its maximum size, so she drew the screen closer, squinting. "I wonder—could that boy be my Opa?"

Commandeering his keyboard, Emma copied and pasted both the image and the link into an email to herself and sent it before she relinquished the tablet. Instead of returning to her books, she shut them, sliding them to the furthest corner of the table.

"I'm not finding anything. Mind if we look together?"

Mind? The only thing he minded was that he had to keep his eyes on the screen. Most of the time. At least this way he could feel the heat of her next to him, her thigh touching his when she leaned.

"Let's start with the easy one." Theo returned to the Family Search website and entered the last name Treager. "What were those dates again?"

She told him, and within seconds he had full birth and death dates as well as a first name. "Ivette Treager. Born 25 Jan. 1862. Died 17 Oct. 1925. Both life events recorded as happening at Indigo Pointe. It has to be her." He glanced at the next closest names, but none of them matched better than Ivette.

"Wow. That was easy. I should have just done that at home."

Emma jotted the information down in a spiral notebook that already included a printed copy of the doorknob photo she'd taken inside the house. It was taped on a page with some other notes in her neat handwriting, and he cringed, remembering when it was taken. If only he hadn't reacted that way. But then again, if he hadn't, she wouldn't be here, sitting beside him. She wouldn't be working for him and he wouldn't see her every day.

"I know you would have, but we just found the

dates a couple of days ago." And she'd been pretty busy with other things. "But I was hoping we'd find something more in those books than we couldn't find online." He shrugged. Apparently libraries weren't all that helpful anymore. "What's next?"

Palms up, she looked for his advice. "The church fire? Did you say you could search back copies of local newspapers?"

"Yes. Let's try that." Theo clicked on the Library of Congress tab to reveal a website with digitized historic American newspapers. He narrowed the search to Louisiana and entered *Indigo Pointe* into the search bar. With less than sixty hits, he decided to go through each, skipping only the ones in French. Articles spoke of everything from crop yields to a fatal accident in the fields. One story caught his eye, and he zoomed in, turning his computer so Emma could read.

"A ball? At Indigo?" Seeing the joy on Emma's face reminded Theo of the lightning bugs several nights before.

"I know. Can you imagine?" A soiree like in the main house's small rooms would have been squished and hot.

"It must have been extraordinary."

Of course they would see it differently. Theo imagined couples chatting on the balconies, all the furniture moved from a room or two so there would be space for dancing. The band could have set up on the back porch. It could have worked.

He watched as Emma clicked through a couple more newspaper articles. Freckles, pale as star shadows, splayed across her nose. "I can't believe how much this family did." *Her* family, she seemed to forget. "They were into everything—government, military, civic groups. In a world without social media, it's amazing how often they ended up in the paper."

"The local newspaper *was* their social media. Ending up in there was one of the hazards or perks, depending on the day, of being part of the wealthy in the community."

"You say that as if it's a good thing," she accused.

Far from it. "No. A fact."

She shook her head, wrinkling her nose. "I don't think I'd ever want to be involved with someone that rich."

"Why not?" His scoff almost sounded like a laugh, but it was far from it. "Because you might get tweeted about?"

She'd have to grow thick skin if she was going to date him. He wasn't famous, at least, but sometimes, by virtue of his money and the obligations—and the privileges, he admitted—that went with the wealth, he ended up being at the kind of events reported in society columns.

"It's not really that so much; it's just not my life." Emma doodled a string of ivy leaves down the side of her notebook. "I think money changes a person. How can people with that kind of cash relate to people like you and me? I mean, I realize you own a plantation and all, but parts of it have been in your family for years. I'm talking about *really* rich people."

"It only changes people who let it." How could he help her understand? "You're saying if this was you." She seemed to be forgetting these were her ancestors they were talking about. "If your family had all this money, you wouldn't want it because it might change you into some terrible stereotype? Think of all the good you could do." He watched her carefully. "All the places you could go." That got a little bit of a reaction. "You can't tell me that doesn't get your little history infatuation bubbling. All the family you could help."

"You make a good point." She completed the ivy chain across the bottom of her page and then went back to perusing the newspaper articles. A couple of silent seconds ticked past. "Wait—" A look of realization crossed Emma's face. "You're one of them, aren't you?"

She'd finally pieced it all together.

While he tried to figure out how to admit she was correct, her eyes grew huge. "I think I found it. Listen to this." She cleared her throat and tried on an official broadcaster voice. "'An incident occurred on Gen.

Bradish Heidel's Indigo Pointe plantation in the parish of St. John the Baptist, last Sunday morning.'"

Theo followed along as she read, distracting himself with the strange capitalization and superfluous commas.

Emma kept reading, but reverted to her usual voice. "'The church, near this Town, caught fire soon after worship services began. Residents of the neighboring plantation rushed to aid in the cessation of the blaze, instituting a water brigade. Sadly, however, our friend, Gen. Heidel and his wife, and two other plantation residents, perished in the fire. The only Heidel family member, a young child, is reported to have survived the incident. Other parishioners seated at the rear of the chapel were able to escape. Many of the Good Samaritans and colored folk who attempted to fight the fire were injured with severe burns, two of the latter, are in precarious conditions.'"

Emma paused to catch a breath. "'The fire was undoubtedly the work of incendiaries, and it is to be hoped that a rigid investigation will disclose the names of the guilty parties, that they may be blasted with the breath of popular indignation.'"

As she read, the news felt like a weight on his chest.

Emma, obviously processing as well, chewed on her bottom lip. "We were right. That's why all those grave markers have the same death year." He thought she might cry, but her voice wobbled on. "They died in the fire. I don't know if I can ever go inside that church again." This time, she was so overcome with emotion, she seemed unable to continue, and Theo knew exactly how she felt.

CHAPTER 19

"Don't be ridiculous, girl."

The voice, like gravel being ground into sidewalk, startled Emma. The woman who'd been practically snoring had awoken to reprimand her?

"That there church fire happened a long time ago—coming up on two centuries more than not. All kinds of Civil War atrocities been happening all over this here parish, and you worried 'bout some unfortunate church fire? If'n you can walk pass them slave quarters y'all have back there, you can go into that church. Gotta be more awful things happened on that property than an accidental fire in a church house. More ghosties in the shadows than in the light."

Emma didn't need to be reminded. The nausea that had gripped her moments ago as she'd read the ledger of St. John the Baptist parish slave sales had made her physically ill.

But this woman had missed the point about the church. "The article said the fire was arson," Emma respectfully challenged.

"You ain't gonna believe a hundred-fifty-year-old paper over the likes of Miss Abbylaide, now is ya? I been around here a lot longer'n you young folk and been hearing all the talk 'bout them good-for-nothin' Lamberts for years, but even I don't believe that."

Emma felt Theo stiffen beside her.

As if preparing for a confrontation with Theo, the woman shifted taller in her seat, and Emma saw the age lines on her face, the experience etched into her features as much as the legends of the land had seeped into her bones. "And I can tell you about the chil' too."

Now this had promise. Theo fidgeted in his seat, so Emma reached over and placed her hand on his, hoping it would calm him.

"I'm so sorry," the woman went on without reacting to Theo. "I been rude. I forgot to introduce myself. I'm Abbylaide Beauchamp of the St. John the Baptist Parish Historical Society." She turned so Emma and Theo could see the dull silver badge pinned to her cardigan. Miss Abbylaide had their full attention and knew it. "The chil' be one Miss Ivette Heidel, three years old."

Miss Abbylaide sure was pleased with herself, but

Emma wasn't sure of the significance of what she was hearing.

"My mama worked for the Treager family for years 'til they sell the place. She cook for the family, always talk about her friend, Miss Ivy, all the time."

"Ivy?" Now that the shock of the tragedy was wearing off, Emma couldn't help but get a little excited. Here was her first real clue. She was sure of it.

"Ivy." The woman smacked her lips loudly. "That's what she go by. Miss Ivy. She never believe the Lamberts start that fire, but you couldn't convince the rest of them Treagers—or that town for that matter."

Emma heard Theo inhale sharply and braced herself. She could feel him seething, and while she had no idea what he was going to say, she knew something was coming.

"So the Treagers blamed the Lamberts for setting the fire?" he asked, his voice cracking subtly. Emma could see Theo's jaw setting. "Was that the genesis of the feud between the families, then?"

Emma turned a look of surprise on Theo. He hadn't said anything about a rift between their families.

"Oh, for sure," Miss Abbylaide said. "Started with them Treagers blaming the Lamberts for setting the fire. Then saying they was trying to take over the house. Nothing worse than them fighting over the house with a little girl caught between. After that the Lamberts sabotage the plantation, making the Treagers lose their house. All part of their plan, them Lamberts, so they could hunt for the Treager treasure. You heard there is treasure on that property, didn't ya?"

Miss Abbylaide turned a squinty eye at Emma. "And now Mr. Lambert gone and done it—took Indigo Pointe away from the rightful owners, I heard. My husband's grandniece, she work at Indigo Pointe—Zoe. She has more right to the place than that Lambert boy." She closed her eyes and shook her head so hard her jowls jiggled with the motion. "Don't get me started …"

"Ms. Beauchamp?" Theo got her attention. "Do you know who I am?"

"Oh, I know 'xactly who you is, Mr. Lambert, but Ms. Treager deserve to know 'xactly who you are and what you's up to as well."

"And what *exactly* do you mean by that?" Theo was barely holding back his temper.

"That you is trying to beat this girl to finding her family treasure."

CHAPTER 20

If that old woman was going to accuse Theo and his family of backhanded, nefarious deeds against a neighbor, Theo was going to stand up to her—even if she was older than Indigo Pointe itself, and by virtue of her age should have earned his respect. Just because she was old or a woman or a human, for that matter, didn't mean she had earned his civility.

He was about to lose the last of his manners when Emma stood and tugged on his hand. He rose, blindly blinking down at the table as he packed up his computer and notes.

"Thank you for sharing the story with us, Miss Abbylaide." Emma was sweeter than freshly powdered beignets. How the woman could be so kind, Theo would never know, but at least Abbylaide Beauchamp had answered all the questions they'd come to the library for.

With his stuff shoved into his messenger bag, Theo turned his back on the table and the person sitting at it.

"'Bye, now," he heard the old woman say. "Good day, Mr. Lambert, Miss Treager." As politely as if she were wishing them well after sharing a glass of iced tea. Well, he didn't like tea, no matter how much sugar you dumped in it, and he felt the same exact way about Miss Abbylaide Beauchamp and her jaded version of his family history. At least she didn't think the Lamberts started the fire.

Emma put a cold hand on his elbow, and the two of them walked from the library. The door to the lobby wasn't even completely closed before she started in. With a sigh. That was the worst, knowing she was disappointed in him.

"What is with you?" Emma's whisper hissed at his side as they marched through the lobby.

"You heard her." He pushed hard on the front door but still took the time to hold it open for her.

"Yes, I did." Emma's words were clipped, staccato accusations against his character. "Are you afraid there might be some truth to her story?"

Coming from Emma, that stung. He could put up with other people, would even been able to blow off

Mrs. Beauchamp's scorn in an hour or two, but he thought Emma knew him better. Apparently not.

"She doesn't know anything about me or my family." He swallowed hard, trying to control his anger. Two deep breaths, and he felt more collected.

Emma stopped and forced him to look at her. "Then why are you so angry?"

"I'm not." While that wasn't exactly true, he also knew she meant more than just today. But she had no idea what it felt like to be judged by everyone for something he hadn't done. In fact, it hadn't even been *his* family; it had been hers. Yet somehow, because he owned the plantation, he was the monster doomed to pay restitution at the hand of public accusation. He fought to earn the upper hand over his fury. How was it that he could care for Emma so much, yet find himself with such a short fuse around her?

"Well, you could have fooled me."

He started walking again, keeping his eyes off her, and focused on where he wanted to go. Hopefully a few yards of silence would lessen the tension.

"You know, Theo, we get to choose what defines us." Emma's tone was softer now, which made him feel even more like a jerk. "If you want to change people's opinions of you, and if you want Indigo Pointe to be successful, you might need to work on your public image."

She was probably trying to tell him he needed to control his temper. He knew this already, but at this point, he really didn't care. If Emma could believe the worst in him, did it matter what everyone else thought? How could she think so little of him when, just nights before, her lips had been pressed against his, her fingertips tracing the muscles at the back of his neck? Didn't she know him well enough to see that his only intention was to help her, no matter what their families' past had been?

To him it had been about their dance in the moonlight and her childlike wonder at the lightning bugs. Shadows and memories turning into beauty and hope.

CHAPTER 21

What am I doing? Emma knew it was embarrassment more than anything else that was bothering her. But could she be with a guy who couldn't hold his temper with an elderly stranger? Or someone who would take his frustrations out on her? Maybe Theo wasn't the man she thought he was.

Her phone buzzed in her purse, and she pulled it out to see her father's photo on the screen.

"Hi, Dad." The crushing pain of disappointment over things with Theo settled behind her eyes, and she pinched the bridge of her nose.

The two of them had reached Theo's truck, and he opened the door for her, silently waiting for her to get in before clicking it closed.

"Hey, chickadee, how's Louisiana?" Her father's voice sounded heavier than usual, but maybe that was her imagination.

So many possible answers ran through her mind, but she went with the expected. "Sticky." It aptly described more than the weather. "What's up?" It wasn't like her father to call during the day in the middle of the week.

"Opa's in the hospital."

She could hear the pain and worry in her father's words and felt them echo in her chest. "Oh no. Is it serious?"

Theo threw a glance of concern her direction. While the last thing she wanted was for him to be dragged into her present-day family drama, there was no way to keep him from overhearing at least her side of the conversation. She put the call on speaker, lifting a finger to her lips as an understanding between them that Theo wasn't to say anything. It would save her from having to explain everything.

"We're not sure how serious his condition is at the moment," her father said. "His heartbeat has been irregular and he's very lethargic." He paused long enough to wipe out the emotion that was leaking through his voice. "Opa hasn't been well for a few days, and Oma is beside herself with worry. She's afraid she's going to lose her husband, which then gets her to worrying about everything else, including saying she'll lose her home trying to pay Opa's medical expenses. I've tried to tell her it's too early to worry about all that, and we'll help take care of things. I know it will all work out."

It sounded as if he needed someone to tell him that, but Emma couldn't. Not when she couldn't see the possibility herself.

"Anyway," her father went on, "I know you haven't been working there long, but do you think your employer would give you time off for a visit?"

Theo nodded emphatically in her peripheral vision.

"Of course I'll come." Emma's mind was spinning one hundred miles per hour. "If he comes home, maybe I should move in to help care for him." She couldn't believe she was saying this. Was it her responsibility to give up her career?

"Oh, honey, I appreciate the offer, but as I said, it's too early to worry about things like that."

"And I'll have a long drive to think about it." Emma couldn't possibly scrape together enough money to fly last-minute. She would feel guilty about leaving her job at Indigo Pointe unfinished, but at least she hadn't broken ground on the new front entrance. "I'll see you soon, Dad. Love you."

Ending the call, Emma slipped the phone into her

purse pocket, a tornado of disorganized plans swirling in her head.

"Let me help." The gentleness was back in Theo's voice, the arguments and tension between them forgotten.

She shook her head. "There's nothing that can be done." She blinked back a few tears. What if Opa passed away before she could get there? Or what if, when she got there, he did end up needing her help? How long could she put her life on hold? What kind of monster did it make her if she didn't?

"At least let me fly you home so you can spend some time with him. Show him pictures of the doorknob and the graves, tell him what you've found so far." Theo didn't say it, but she felt he was implying it would give her grandfather a reason to hang on until his hundredth birthday and the solution to his mystery.

Theo was sincere, Emma assured herself. This wasn't a manipulation after their argument. He wasn't looking for any kind of quid pro quo. He wasn't trying to buy her forgiveness, was he?

This was exactly the reason she wouldn't ever be with a rich guy, not if she always wondered about ulterior motives. Her mind hurt trying to parse it all out. She leaned her head into her hands, allowing the blast of air conditioning to blow her hair from her face, unsure what to do.

"One phone call and I could have a plane ready to take off in an hour, hour and a half. Please?" Theo touched her arm, his hand gentle and reassuring. "Go for a few days, spend time with your loved ones." He seemed to perceive the cause of her worry. "If you end up needing to return home permanently, we'll figure it out then." He rubbed her back in small circles as he drove. "Try to take it one step at a time."

Exhaustion flooded through her; the worry and stress, both physical and emotional, was taking its toll. There was no way she could start that drive today. "Okay."

Emma leaned back and closed her eyes. She imagined herself back in Theo's arms, the two of them the only people in their own private, magical garden of fireflies. She wanted nothing more than to allow him to take care of her just this once. She was beginning to feel she'd been all wrong about her assumptions about Theo and rich men.

She relaxed into the headrest and fell asleep until Theo woke her in the parking lot at Indigo Pointe.

CHAPTER 22

Emma had only been gone a couple of days, but it felt like forever to Theo. He'd planned to throw himself back into work, which had been his MO before he'd ever met Emma, but instead, he wandered aimlessly around Indigo Pointe. What he needed to do was to set up some face-to-face meetings in Nice and Budapest, but for the first time in his life, the deserts of eastern Oregon had more of a pull on his mind and heart than the hillsides of Europe. Something he'd never expected to happen.

Emma had taken Theo's view on life and turned it just enough that he could see another perspective. It was because of her, his life was more rich and full than money could ever hope to make it, and without her, he could feel the shadows creeping back in. Her hasty departure on the heels of their first misunderstanding made the exquisite times together pale. Where were things between them? He wanted to call her, hear her voice happy as if filled with wildflowers, but he knew she'd been going home to worry, illness, and financial strain, and he couldn't bear to hear the weight of it pulling her down. He had to help her—not for the sake of mending their relationship, but because he loved her and wanted to ease her burden.

Had he really just thought that? He loved her?

He headed for the rose garden, the place he felt closest to Emma after their shared lesson and laughs. The last time he'd been there, the two of them had trimmed the dying rosebushes back so far he expected to see nothing more than bare plants struggling to recuperate. Now when he passed under the arched arbor, he was greeted with strings of tiny buds like Christmas lights stretched across the fence rails, ready to burst open at any moment. Evidence that the woman had a positive influence on every aspect of his life. His arms ached to hold her.

"They look great," Zoe said from behind him. "She's amazing, isn't she?"

He knew Zoe wasn't expecting an answer, not that he could have given one. "I want to do something for her. Do you have any ideas?" He'd given it a lot of thought since Emma's departure. "I wanted to gift her the plantation, put it back into the Treager family, but I can't leave her with the renovation expenses and a huge tax bill."

"Maybe not that," Zoe agreed, "but you've done so much for her already." Zoe cupped her hands around one of the new rosebuds and breathed in deeply before looking back at Theo. "By employing her here, you've provided a connection with her ancestors she never would have had. You allow her creative control and an opportunity to improve the family homestead. You're considering hiring her brother as general contractor for a huge job. You're giving them the best parts of their history, and I didn't think you could beat that, but you did."

Zoe turned her full attention back to Theo. "You have no idea how grateful she was for you flying her home—you should have heard about her gush over the private jet. I'm thinking you didn't prepare her for that?" Zoe's eyes twinkled with amusement.

Theo smiled, glad he'd been able to be of assistance and surprise her at the same time. "Thanks for driving her out there."

"The girl had no idea how much you're worth. I thought she was more observant than that, but I guess you did a decent job of hiding it."

"It didn't come up until it was too late." Theo was

glad it hadn't backfired worse than it did at the library. What was he supposed to have done, flaunt his wealth and brag about his holdings? They'd barely begun getting to know each other. It hadn't come up naturally, and by the time he knew her feelings on the subject, pretty much the next thing he'd done was fly her on a private jet. "I guess the cat's out of the bag now, though."

"Yeah, she kind of pumped me for details until I broke."

It probably hadn't been that hard. "How'd she take it?" Theo felt like lightning bugs were trapped in his chest, wriggling to escape.

"Surprised."

"Good surprised or bad surprised?" This was killing him.

"Not sure." Zoe had a teasing twinkle in her eye. "Maybe you should call her."

"Great. Thanks for the help."

"Any time." Zoe laughed. "I wouldn't worry, Theo. Be your kind, sweet self. Let her know you're thinking about her, and everything will work out okay."

That only made him feel worse. Emma hadn't responded to his first text asking about her trip, and he'd decided to give her space, a little time to herself before he tried again. But he did need to follow up with

Emma's brother, Brett. Maybe Brett would help him with a few errands.

"That gives me an idea." The lightning bugs settled down as he formulated a plan. "Thanks for the help."

This time he meant it.

CHAPTER 23

Emma rested her great-grandfather's journal on her lap, open to the page with the sketch of the metalwork on Opa's wooden stationary box. She had examined the box in person as soon as she'd had the chance, but reading through her Opa's father's journal again had helped her realize that the box was more than a starting point. It might actually be the end.

Opa snorted softly in his sleep, waking himself up. Now that he was home again, his favorite place to sleep was his recliner, though he fought with the locking mechanism several times a day.

Emma shuffled the journal off her lap and jumped up to help Opa, easing the recliner backward until it locked. "Better?"

"Thank you, darlin'." He gave her a weak smile. "It is so nice having you here for a few days. I know your Oma appreciates it too."

"It's nice being home." Though that was true at first, it was becoming less so. They'd had this conversation more than a couple of times already. "I never thought I'd say this in the heat of the summer, but Nyssa is so much cooler than Louisiana."

"You got that right," he agreed heartily. "I'll never forget those hot summer nights sleeping with the windows open on both sides of the house to try to get a breeze." Theo had mentioned that very practice in his tour speech. "Tell me more about your new job."

"I'm the landscape architect at Indigo Pointe Plantation." She wanted to make it sound as prestigious as possible so she didn't get accused of being a "glorified gardener," as her father had joked.

"Indigo Pointe." Opa closed his eyes, a look of deep contentment settling on his face as if reliving pleasant memories. "Yes, that's the name."

"Yes, and it would have helped if you had remembered that. Would have made my job finding it a ton easier," she teased.

As he chuckled, the crinkles around his eyes deepened for a second. "And where would the fun in that be?" He pointed to the journal sitting beside her. "I gave you a pretty good starting point, though, didn't I?"

Now it was her turn to be overwhelmed with fond memories. "You're right. Theo and I have had a good time unraveling the clues."

"Who's this Theo?" Opa got that look older people get when they were matchmaking.

"Theo Lambert. He's my boss." As soon as she'd said it, she wished she hadn't pointed out that little fact.

His expression changed like an incoming thunderstorm, quick and unmistakable. "Lambert, did you say?"

Emma nodded.

"So that gold-digging family finally succeeded in taking the place away from us, did they? That's what they always wanted."

Emma hadn't heard her grandfather grumble much in his life, and she wouldn't allow him to start, especially when he didn't know Theo. "If he hadn't bought it, the plantation would have been rubble within a decade. He has plans to restore it."

"Don't let him fool you. He's just after the treasure."

She couldn't believe the vitriol seeping from her grandfather. "He's a good man, Opa."

Now that she'd separated from Theo and allowed herself to ponder on the library scene and the ensuing argument, she realized not only had he had every right to feel defensive, but she missed him.

And now she might have lost him. Thinking back on her tirade about money, embarrassment washed over her again. Had she really been that blind? How she hadn't noticed his circumstances was baffling, except that she'd made assumptions, seen what she'd wanted to see. Apparently she had some prejudices she'd needed to examine. If Theo was rich, and obviously he was, she'd certainly had it all wrong.

"All I know is that family has been trying to steal the place from us for nigh on two centuries now."

It was easy to dismiss Opa when he made blanket statements like that. She knew Theo and was sure of his motivations. He was kind and generous and real.

Emma picked up the journal and thumbed through it again. Something didn't add up, and she was surprised she hadn't thought of it before. "If there's actual treasure, Opa, why didn't your family use it to keep the plantation instead of selling?"

"Because we have no idea where it is."

"And neither does Theo." Emma didn't want to argue with her grandfather, but she wouldn't allow his prejudice to be *her* stumbling block. "Have you ever thought," she added as kindly as she could, "that maybe the treasure isn't actually at Indigo Pointe?" Opa's face grew hard as he considered it, and she hurried on, "I mean, if it were there somewhere, someone should have found it by now."

He didn't say anything, so she decided to switch tactics. "Do you remember much about your grandmother, Ivette Treager?"

"A little." His face softened again. Watching it vacillate with his moods was like watching a weather vane switch back and forth in a storm.

"I have a picture you might want to see." She went to her bag to pull out the photos she'd had printed—the gravestone, the doorknob, and the one Theo had found online of the people in front of the church. She handed them over, along with his reading glasses, and sat back to tell him everything she'd learned so far.

CHAPTER 24

Theo completed the last of his calls and plugged in his dying phone. Noise from the busy French Quarter dissuaded him from opening the balcony doors, but at least it was calm in his house. Theo picked up Emma's impromptu sketch from their gumbo dinner, a talisman he'd taken to looking at as a way to look back on their time together. He sank into his butter-soft leather couch and turned on some Rachmaninoff to relax. Putting the plan into motion had taken more work than he'd expected at the outset, but the payoff was going to be well worth his time. All that was left now as he waited for Emma to come back to Louisiana was to see if there was anything more for him to glean about the Treager family treasure.

The main house at Indigo Pointe was completely

bereft of bookshelves, pointing back to the fact that the home had been more of a showpiece on the outside rather than offering true luxury inside. Theo had scoured the entire property. There were no hidden tunnels, cubbyholes, or niches behind paintings. No jewelry boxes or chests or valuable tapestries. Now that he'd searched everything at Indigo Pointe, all that was left were the family journals. Perhaps he could uncover another clue, another perspective of the goings-on at Indigo Pointe.

The wall of books in his home, artfully arranged by the interior decorator, was overwhelming, but after fifteen minutes of pulling out random books and going up and down ladders, Theo finally found a shelf with some potential. A few privately published family hardbacks accompanied handwritten journals and some loose papers, contracts scrawled on brittle paper, tucked in for safekeeping. Tired after a long day, Theo chose one of the typeset histories as his starting place.

Theo settled in with it, breathing in the scent of the old book and feeling the heft of it in his hands, wondering why he didn't do this more often. He skimmed over boring things like planting schedules and rainfalls, droughts and yields. It read like an almanac: dry and, for his purposes, useless. He'd just found an account of the fire when his phone rang with Emma's ringtone.

Could it be? He answered quickly, eager to hear her voice again.

After a few shy niceties on both sides, Emma nudged their conversation to the point of her call. "Could I ask a favor?" She seemed hesitant. What would it take for her to trust that he'd do anything for her? "Looks like the family has decided to move up Opa's hundredth birthday party a couple of months. They don't think he'll notice, and it feels safer than waiting, in case he takes a turn for the worse. Besides, since it's summer, there's not as much to do on the farm right now as there will be in the fall."

She was cute when she rambled. He already knew this was coming, but he was enjoying talking with her and stretched it out as long as possible.

"I was thinking of staying here for another week or two before heading back to Indigo Point, if that's okay. Don't worry, I've been working on the design for the front drive. I think you're going to like it."

Of course he would. Everything she did was beautiful. And of course he'd rather have her back in Louisiana with him, but he could wait. She needed this time. Her whole family did.

"It's really not a problem, Emma. I've got a lawn crew from Contrary Mary's trying to maintain what you started. Zoe's keeping them on task. The projects you haven't started yet can wait until you return." Because, more than anything, he wanted her to come back. "And when you're ready, I won't need much notice to get the plan to you. The pilot might appreciate a day's notice, but he's flexible."

Were things only going to be business between them now? He ached to pour his heart out to her, but felt it was too soon. He needed to allow time for his plan to be carried out.

"Thank you, Theo." Her tone was a caress, and he felt the ache lessen, especially as she continued. "I knew I could count on you."

While it wasn't the easy banter he missed so much, it was a start. "See you soon." Clicking over to speaker, Theo pulled up her contact picture so he could say goodbye to her face to face. How he missed her smile and the librarian glasses. "Enjoy your family. I'm glad your grandfather is doing better."

Theo wanted to say more and wished he had another clue to share with her. Given another five minutes, he might have, but he didn't want to bring up this mention of the fire until he knew he had something new.

He hung up and reluctantly closed the image of Emma, returning to the account of the fire from his own great-great-grandfather's point of view. Afterward, as directed by the account, Theo flipped through one handwritten journal after another until he found a velvet ribbon, green so dark it was almost black, tied to a long, thin key with a miniature head. The same distinct ivy design was stamped in the brass. He'd found it, even had an idea what the key might unlock, and he knew exactly what had to come next.

CHAPTER 25

Emma didn't know for certain who hired Macy, the party planner, but she was worth her weight in sugar beets. Emma especially appreciated that having Macy took so much stress off Oma, who wouldn't allow her kids to take over the party but was more than willing to relinquish the planning to the energetic Macy.

While Emma worried about the expense, no one else seemed concerned, so she sat back into a turquoise tulle-wrapped chair to watch as Macy added the final touches to Opa's hundredth birthday celebration. How Macy had organized everything so quickly and flawlessly, Emma didn't expect to ever discover, but she was impressed that it even included arranging travel for family who Emma had thought would be too far away to attend.

It had always been the plan that the large barn between Opa's house and Uncle Linus's would be the venue, and Macy had transformed it into a country chic affair, Pinterest-worthy in every way. Round tables with lacy tablecloths dotted the room but left a generous dance floor near the live band set up in one corner. Balloons and flowers brightened the area, and a chocolate fountain bubbled in expectation. While she had a sneaking suspicion who hired Macy and had paid Opa's medical bills, it wasn't until Emma smelled gumbo and muffalettas for the buffet fare that she knew it had to be him.

"Hey, sis." Brett grabbed the chair next to Emma and turned it around backward before sitting down. He had a bowlful of rice and gumbo and was eating as if he hadn't had a decent meal in weeks. His wife, Afton, sat beside him, smiling like a mother indulging an overactive child.

"How's Chicago?" Although it had been months since Emma had seen them, she loved how it never felt like there was a gulf between her and her brother.

"It's a pretty sweet gig, but it's only a few more months." He gave an apologetic look to Afton, and Emma realized she shouldn't have brought it up. All the moving around couldn't be easy for the rest of the family.

"How about this party? What a shindig. I didn't expect it to be this nice." He took a swig of lemonade. "I guess Aunt Cheryl wasn't in charge."

Emma agreed.

"How's the new job?" Brett asked.

Emma tried to pretend things were strictly professional when she felt anything but that about Theo. "I love it."

"Umm-hmm." Brett took another bite, savored it, and then swallowed. "Why don't I believe you're talking about Indigo Pointe?" He reached over to squeeze Afton's hand as if sharing a secret. "If I didn't know you better, sis, I might think you care for this Theo Lambert."

It didn't escape her notice that he knew Theo's name without her saying it. Opa must have told him. "Maybe I do." She gave Brett her best "challenge me" look, but he merely grinned like a guilty beagle caught digging up the onions.

"Good, because the guy just offered me a job."

"That's great!" Emma was thrilled.

Wait, *just* offered him a job—did he mean literally? Emma took a long sip of her raspberry lemonade, allowing her gaze to roam around the crowded barn. Brett must have meant on the phone. Her eyes settled on a gnome in a LSU jersey standing as a doorstop. Had that been there before? It couldn't have been.

Emma stood, looking from person to person until her eyes locked on Theo Lambert's. As soon as she found him, he started wending his way cautiously toward her, a half smile on his face.

She rushed to him and threw her arms around his neck, kissing his stubbly cheek. "You came!"

He looked amazing in his tux, and she stepped back to admire him.

"Of course I came." The cleft in his chin deepened as he smiled. "I'll always come for you."

She took in the sight of him, relieved he wasn't a mirage. "I still can't believe you're here."

Her eyes lingered on his lips, just for a moment, but she decided to postpone that, bringing him in for another hug. "Thank you," she whispered into his neck, so choked up she could hardly get the words out. "For everything." She stepped back and motioned to the room.

"It truly is my pleasure."

Emma could tell that he meant it. She had to lighten the mood before she either burst into tears or kissed him thoroughly. "I knew it had to be you. Who else would dress a poor, defenseless gnome in yellow and purple?"

He took her hand, gazing silently into her eyes for a

moment before leading her through the crowd to the front door. "I have something for you." From his jacket pocket, he pulled out a ribbon long enough to be worn as a necklace that ended in a knot around a sliver of a brass key.

Reverently, she accepted the key, turning it over in her palm. "It matches exactly."

"Any chance we could try it?"

It only took her a moment to realize he meant the stationary box. "Now?" Her heart hammered with anticipation.

"I don't think anyone will miss us."

She slipped the key around her neck to free up her hand, which she fit into Theo's. Walking down a dirt road perhaps wasn't the most elegant setting, but the mint scent rising from the field next to them was soothing.

"Brett said you offered him a job." A hot, dry breeze played at the hem of her skirt.

"He mentioned that he and his wife had always talked about renovating a house of their own, and I was thinking of offering him the church to fix up how they want. Is that weird?"

There was her sweet, unsure Theo again. She squeezed his hand. "He would *love* that."

"And would that be okay with you?"

"Me?" Why would he ask her that? Why wouldn't it

be? Why would she have any say? "Of course." Theo's generosity astounded her, though she shouldn't have been surprised. "Imagine how relieved Oma was when she got word from both the hospital and the bank that all debts were paid, and with quite a bit of padding to take care of them."

Theo seemed to be judging her reaction. As if she could be upset. She stopped and turned to face him. "I'm so relieved. We all are." Her lips had suddenly gone dry, and she licked them quickly. "Thank you. From all of us."

Theo fell silent for a moment. "Does that mean you'll come back to Indigo with me, Emma?"

Was he really afraid she wouldn't want to come back to him? After what she'd said about rich men, she could understand his uncertainty.

She took both of his hands in hers, threading their fingers together and taking a long moment to look deeply into his sparkling lake-blue eyes. When she spoke, her voice was a whisper. "I knew it. You really need my expertise in the gardens, don't you?"

Theo let out a surprised chuckle. "No. I mean, yes, but that's not why I want you back. I want to take you on fancy dates and spend time with you under the stars. I want to take you to Europe so you can get inspiration for our landscaping, and then I want to come back and implement your designs. Whatever, whenever it is, I want to do it with you."

She leaned in, brushing her lips against his. "That sounds amaz—"

Before allowing her to finish what she was saying, Theo's lips were on hers again, soft and strong, full of hope and promise, whirling her away from Oregon, Louisiana, or anywhere else she could picture. It was just the two of them, absent of time or place, taking full advantage of being in each other's arms again.

After several long kisses, Emma stepped back. "I thought we had a box to find." She lifted the key and waved it as a reminder.

Theo, however, didn't seem to be watching it. His eyes hadn't left her face, and his expression said he hadn't wanted to step away from the kiss either. "Did I mention that after you finish the landscaping at Indigo Pointe, I have a few other homes you could take a look at? They might need makeovers as well."

She narrowed her eyes at him, seeming to think about it. "I'll do the designs, but we're hiring someone to do the labor."

He screwed up his lips, his turn in the negotiation to consider. "I'll have to check with my accountant, but I think we could make that work."

She grabbed his hand again and turned, tugging him

toward the house. "Come on. I want to see if there's a place for this key."

In the end, instead of turning the key themselves, Emma and Theo decided it was Opa's to try. They made the trip back to the party, box in hand, eager to see if anything would come of it.

"Opa, Oma." Emma found them at the head table, talking with Emma's parents and aunt and uncle. She set the box on the table in front of her grandparents. "This is Theo Lambert," she introduced quickly, skimming over the ritual, "and he found something that just might have solved our mystery."

Opa's green-and-brown hazel eyes, so like her own, sparkled in anticipation. "Yes?"

Emma took the key from her neck and handed it to him. "See how it has the same design as ours?"

Opa tried to look at it, but gave up after a couple of seconds. "I'll take your word for it." He chuckled. "My eyes aren't what they used to be."

Emma's dad reached over and took it from him, briefly running a thumb over the ivy design. "A perfect match." He handed it back to his father. "Try it."

After thoroughly examining the box with its compartments and hinges, none of them could figure out where the key would go.

"But there isn't a place for it." Oma voiced the disappointment they all felt.

"What if you inserted it in the regular keyhole?" Emma suggested. While their slightly larger key worked the lock to the hinged doors on the box, Emma supposed it was possible this thinner key would turn a tumbler behind the first.

With shaky hands, Opa inserted the tiny key. With a half twist, a click sounded and a hidden drawer popped free at the base. Sliding the drawer open, Opa pulled out a single sheet of yellowed parchment and handed it to Emma. "Read it for us?"

With a nervous laugh, Emma accepted the paper. "Of course you'd want me to read it," she grumbled under her breath. The handwriting, however, was thankfully perfectly legible.

Our dearest Ivy—

Only Divine Intervention could have placed you in our lives at the time we needed each other the most. In the midst of tragedy, one amazing miracle occurred. You were that miracle.

On March 26, 1865, while you attended worship services with your family and the plantation staff, a fire overtook the church building. Seeing the smoke, we, your neighbors, rushed to put out the fire. While we were able to stop the outside of the building from burning completely, the inside was so engulfed, it was impossible to save anyone. Thankfully, many souls were able to escape the ravages of the flames, yet providence didn't shine on all in the building, and sadly some perished.

In the chaos of those trying to fight the fire, you, a small child of three, were found scratched and bleeding in the rose bushes, having been tossed out the window by, we can only assume, well-meaning parents in an attempt to save your young life. One of the kitchen help discovered you, recognized your sobbing through the tumult of the fire, and brought you to us for safekeeping.

While it is true we saved your life that day, you saved ours as well. Our hearts ached for your tremendous loss, that of your parents and siblings—everyone you loved in your short life. We tended the burns on your skin and the scorching pain in your heart.

You, in turn, gave us the opportunity to be parents when our arms ached for a baby of our own. The plan was to do our Christian duty and care for you, the offspring of our estranged neighbor, until your closest kin would come and accept not only the responsibility of Indigo Pointe but your care as well. What we didn't realize was that we would fall in love with you as the daughter we had longed for.

After an extended absence, your distant cousin, Mr. Treager, and his family arrived at Indigo Pointe. By that time, you had been living in our household for six years. In that time you had become a daughter, a big sister (finally!), and in every way but name, a Lambert, but that was not to be your future.

Knowing Mr. Treager was coming to claim you and Indigo Pointe, as was his right and responsibility, we have decided to leave reminders of our love for you where you will see them every day—symbols that remind us as well of our precious Ivy who will always be in our hearts. So when you see the ivy motifs on this box and around your home at Indigo Pointe, know that even though we cannot be physically with you, our love always will be.

It is with heavy hearts that we return the true treasure of Indigo Pointe—you, our dear, sweet Ivy. We hope and pray that the Treager family will care for you and love you as we have done. We will always watch over you, our dear Ivy, and you will always be in our hearts.

Mr. & Mrs. Giles Lambert

When Emma finished reading, she looked about the table, gauging reactions. Theo looked calm but pensive. Her parents shushed Brett's daughter, Talia, on Emma's mom's lap. She focused on Opa last of all.

"Ivy, my grandmother, was the Treager treasure?" Opa's shock was representative of the group. "That wasn't what I was expecting. How about you, Mr. Lambert? Did your family know?" He looked to Theo for an answer.

Theo shook his head and let out a quick cough of a laugh. "If we're being honest here, no, this is what I'd been raised to expect either." He seemed to be considering his words carefully. "I wish I knew how our families got the story so confused. Perhaps the Lamberts thought Indigo Pointe should have been theirs because they'd run the plantation between the time of the fire and the coming of Mr. Treager, but the treasure being a person?" He paused. "No. I had no idea, and I don't think my father did, either."

Opa nodded, accepting the explanation. A few quiet minutes, and Opa's eyes misted. "I remember Ivy. I was young, of course, but my mother spoke kindly of her as well. Ivy was always so loving to everyone around her—especially the Lamberts—and now we know why." His look at Theo was one of gratitude, not the contempt Emma had seen when he'd talked about the Lambert family before. Opa stopped. "But wait. How was Ivy a Treager? I thought it was through marriage."

True. Ivy had been the daughter of Mr. and Mrs. Heidel, who'd died in the church fire that day.

"I can shed some light on that," Theo offered. "I found an entry in my great-great-grandfather's journal the other night, something I thought was a bit strange for him to record. It was an account of one Miss Ivette Heidel, aged seventeen, being married to her cousin, the son of Mr. Arthur Treager, the distant relative who had taken over Indigo Pointe after the fire. My relative never explained the fire, mentioning it as if anyone reading would already know the circumstances. What he did say was that the son, who married his parents' young charge, had been away at school in Massachusetts all that time and had never even met Ivette until not long before their union. It would seem he was a bit older than Ivy?" This was a question he directed at Opa, who nodded.

Theo continued, "It sounds like it was all on the up and up. The Lamberts took seriously their self-proclaimed mission to watch over Ivy even after she'd gone to live with the Treagers, though I didn't understand the context before this letter."

Emma handed the letter to Opa, who clutched it to his chest. "You solved the mystery." His relief and joy were evident. He took in both Emma and Theo with a thankful gaze. "I knew there was something special about this box, but I had no idea it had come from the Lamberts. And contained the . . . treasure map."

"So really both families did want the same thing after all—the happiness and well-being of Ivy." Emma sighed, content with the news that the Lamberts hadn't been after the plantation, hadn't caused the fire, and had done everything and more that good neighbors would do.

Opa stood, hand outstretched to Theo. "Will you forgive me?"

"Absolutely, sir." Theo squirmed in the center of everyone's attention. "There's nothing to forgive."

"Thank you for rescuing Indigo Pointe," Opa said, his eyes on Theo while he patted Emma's arm. "All I ask is that you take good care of her."

Emma was fairly certain Opa meant the plantation *and* his granddaughter.

CHAPTER 26

Emma and Theo walked the grounds of the Indigo Pointe Plantation for the first time since coming back to Louisiana. Emma allowed Theo to lead her through the arbor, knowing he wanted to check on his favorite roses; she'd been curious to see them herself. Emma was relieved to see they'd flourished in their absence. "Looks like they survived, even with my meddling," she teased him, remembering all too well how reticent he'd been when he first saw her touching them.

"I'm glad you meddled." Using his pocketknife, Theo cut one of the champagne roses, the head full and fragrant, and handed it to her. "A rose for my beauty."

He took her hand again, and she followed him toward her garçonnière. Twilight had set in, and while the fireflies were disappointingly absent, the background symphony of katydids, crickets, and an occasional frog serenaded them home.

Jet lag tugged at Emma's eyes so much that she almost didn't recognize the lump on the front step as a new gnome. "Do you know what I know about gardens in Europe?"

"What?" Theo's voice was husky in the darkness.

"Not one single gnome."

Theo smiled and raised their clasped hands to his lips, brushing a kiss across her knuckles, but her eyes were on the gnome, trying to determine its shape. A glint of light sparkled. Something shiny was in the large sunflower the gnome held over his head.

"A ring?" Emma reached forward to pick it up, a large-carat cushion-cut diamond sparkled in a vintage setting. It was gorgeous.

"And a gem for my Treager treasure," he said.

Emma turned to find Theo on one knee.

"Emma Treager, would you do me the honor of allowing me to be your husband, so we can cultivate gardens wherever we go?"

Unable to trust herself to speak without choking up, Emma nodded.

With their eyes seeing nothing but each other, Theo gently removed the ring from Emma's fingertips and slipped it halfway onto her finger. "So no objections to becoming a Lambert?" he teased.

She giggled. "I am the one who would be honored."

"I love you, Emma." He trailed kisses from her ear to her lips, the warmth of his breath rushing over her. "All of my love for all of my life."

ACKNOWLEDGMENTS

Building a book is a lot like building a house. You need the creativity and expertise in many diverse technical and professional fields. Where I needed help, I brought in consultants, and this time around, they are many. Just know, that although I am sure they gave me sound and professional advice, if there are any mistakes, I probably either didn't ask the right questions, didn't quite understand what I was told, or completely ignored the advice given because it didn't work with the story (because I'm that kind of rebel). But please accept my sincere thanks, even if I messed it up:

To Tricia Stadler, who has spent many years in a hospital emergency department as an RN (and studying to be a PA), thank you for the ER advice. Despite the fact that I used very little of what I asked you, I appreciate your advice on Avery's possible injuries.

Thank you also to Paul Hirst, a principal architect at Oldham Hirst Design, who answered random questions about blueprints.

Speaking of construction, a big thank you to Tim Bouck, a builder for David Weekly Homes, who answered questions about the process and terminology. If only I'd known the right questions to ask, I'm sure my story would have been even more accurate.

And to my resident Corpus Christi expert, Nichole Giles, thanks for letting me pick your brain for details and setting ideas. It's been a few too many years for me to remember since I was there, and I appreciated having someone to ask.

It was fabulous working with Trifecta Books and the other authors of the Countdown to Christmas novellas. I'm humbled and thrilled to have my book among yours. And thank you to my readers. Without you, there would be little reason to write. Merry Christmas, friends!

As always, a huge thank you to my plot brainstorming crew, my family. You are my best sounding board and never fail to extricate me when I get stuck. I rely on your support, encouragement, and ideas. Thank you, Curtis, Alex, Courtney, and Bennett. Thanks for letting me talk through it until it was written. (And after.)

ABOUT THE AUTHOR

When Maria Hoagland is not working at her computer, she can be found combing used furniture stores and remodeling houses with her husband. She loves crunching leaves in the fall, stealing cookie dough from the mixing bowl, and listening to musicals on her phone.

Maria has several published works in the sweet romance and women's fiction genres. She enjoys hearing from readers and book clubs and can be found online at mariahoagland.com.

For updates on new releases and a free copy of the novella *New Year's Resolutions*, sign up for Maria's newsletter on her website.

- facebook.com/mariahoaglandauthor
- twitter.com/MariaHoagland
- instagram.com/mariahoagland
- bookbub.com/authors/maria-hoagland
- pinterest.com/mariahoagland

NEXT IN THE BILLIONAIRE CLASSICS SERIES

Thank you for reading *Beauty & the Billionaire Beast!*

Continue your journey into rewrites of favorite classic novels that will have you falling in love again and again. Billionaire Classics are three interconnected contemporary sweet romances inspired by classic literature that can be enjoyed alone.

Her App, a Match, and the Billionaire

Seattle's exclusive neighborhood The Cove is the setting for this Jane Austen-inspired *Pride & Prejudice* reimagining.

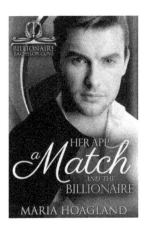

Falling for Her Billionaire Best Friend

Seattle's Cove takes on unexpected twist inspired by Lewis Carroll's *Alice's Adventures in Wonderland.*

CPSIA information can be obtained
at www.ICGtesting.com
Printed in the USA
LVHW030105240420
654346LV00001B/67